NOTES ON FALLING

The following work is a work of fiction. Names, characters, places, and incidents either are the product of the author's imagination or are used fictitiously. Any resemblance to actual persons, living or dead, events, or locales is entirely coincidental.

Notes on Falling

Published by
Twit Publishing
Dallas, Texas

Edited by Chris Gabrysch

First Edition paperback 2012

Dedication Space

Contents

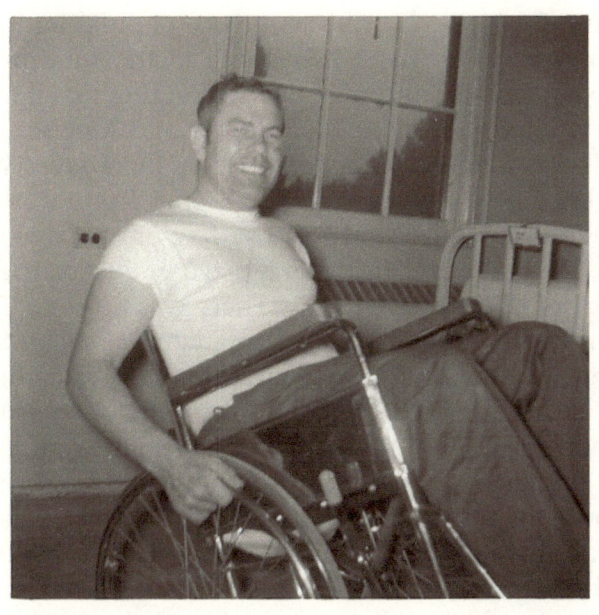

I Think This Is When It All Started

1

My father was a welder. He was the guy that walked around on the I-beams way up in the air and welded the structural skeletons of buildings together. It was a tortuous job in the broiling Texas sun. It was a numbing, miserable livelihood in the grey, stark, silent death of February, especially when the blue northers bore their wrath from the unsympathetic Midwest. It was always dirty. It was always dangerous. It required men with special strengths and few weaknesses.

Back in '59 there was a lot of work going around, and it was catching. We needed airports for the growing airline industry. Country clubs became very popular and needed to be built. There was a new thing in the suburbs called "shopping centers" and they were springing up all over the country. There was money to be spent and America needed stuff. It was a time of change; different than now. We were at the beginning of a new way of living. There was no fast food yet, just "Dairy Mart" and a few other drive-in-type places. We had never heard of a pizza or a taco. There was Frostie Root Beer *and* Triple X! There was no color TV, and when it finally got here a few years later, at six on Sunday evening was the only program filmed and transmitted in "living color." A pack of cigarettes was about thirty cents and they'd sell 'em to you if you said they were for your mom. We spent all Saturday morning watching cartoons. Just imagine, no Super Bowl, and yet we still managed to get by. But we did have some things nearly as entertaining though, like screen doors. And, as if that wasn't enough excitement, we had folk music and beatniks. We had sonic booms. You could actually walk into a store and tell the clerk to "put it on your bill." I'm sure you already heard the one about milk being delivered (that one gets me every time). Doughnuts were sold warm door to door, and blind men with their dogs hawked household cleaners and brushes right on your doorstep. Nobody that *you* knew had ever gotten high on "goofballs." A man would come by every so often and sharpen your kitchen knives and scissors. Now, you tell me if this makes more sense, back then your doctor came to *you* if you were sick. All phones in the world were black and they were kept in the hall. Airplanes had something you could actually see working to keep you up in the air. The British had only invaded once in those days. The Silver Beatles were still The Quarrymen. Santa Claus was real. Brian Wilson and his family and friends were doing a very white version of doo-wop (almost a grooving barbershop kind-o-thing, except that "grooving" hadn't been invented yet). Perry Como and Eddie Fisher's careers had taken a nosedive because of that son-of-a-bitch, negra-loving, hip-wigglin, pretty boy from down south, Mr. Pat Boone. For the first time Detroit and Memphis were the places to be for cutting-edge music. In New York City you could see *real* families walking in their "Sunday best" to church on Sunday mornings. It was just another small town, only larger. The Japanese were still "Japs," and they made absolutely *the* cheapest shit you'd ever laid your hands on. Sears sold musical instruments, motorcycles, and everything in between. You could *rent* an ax for fifty cents a day. They would put something called Ethyl in your car to make it go. Kids called other kids "shit-asses" and "buttholes," but without a doubt the worst word ever uttered by any child was the feared "Stickers!" A really nice house cost about $15,000. A man was king of his castle, his word was still his bond, and it was a long, long way from Texas to California.

My father took a job in Los Angeles, California, that year (that's the place where they kept Jerry Lewis and Bob Hope). It was the first time I remember him ever leaving for *any* reason. I didn't really know where California was, even though Bugs Bunny was always singing about it. Being four years old I had no concept of time, so two months meant nothing to me. All I really knew was that you had to wait forever for Christmas to come, and that's all that really mattered anyway, right? So I guess his leaving was really no big deal to me at the time.

My father and a crew of men left Dallas in a convoy of assorted trucks with trailers, tool vans, mobile welding trucks, and the old-style construction cranes mounted on large trucks and marked "WIDE LOAD." The trip took his crew four days, and most of it was spent on the old Route 66. Now being familiar with the route, I can't imagine that the trip between Amarillo and L.A. had much to offer the Texans in the way of sightseeing, especially when you take into account everything was still in black and white back then. I don't know, maybe they thought the Putrefied Forest was cool, maybe not.

My younger brother Kelley had been born a little bit before my dad left. I remember thinking that my mother was pregnant all my life with him. We waited for years and years and all we got was — Kelley; talk about a letdown. All he ever did was cry and pee and that was it, the full extent of his talents, crying and peeing. Oh yeah, he was *really* worth the wait.

My other brother Gary was six years older than I was, so he was already all grown up. He was handsome, funny, athletic, smart, and popular in school. I, being "retarded," was a constant source of entertainment for Gary and his friends. I would routinely have acts of torture performed upon me. I swear to you, there were actually human sacrifices carried out for their amusement. I'm *really* not kidding about this. Sure my older brother and his friends killed a bunch of people back then, someone should check this out — but don't tell 'em I'm the one that told you.

Ya know what *really* sucks? *Both* my brothers can kick my ass. When my little brother was born I thought, "Oh cool, now I have a little brother that *I* can hurt." That's how the system works, right? Well no, this new kid came right out of the womb six foot two and 270 pounds. I never got to hit him even once. Life is unfair.

Oh yeah, by the way, just for the record, did I mention my sister Susie? Yeah, she can kick my ass too.

Anyway, I'm sure my father kissed me goodbye when he left, but I don't remember. Then he was gone. He went "far away for a long time." You should remember, back then Fort Worth was far away, and nap-time was a long time. Although even now Fort Worth is still pretty far back in time. I don't think I understood what was *really* going on. I don't know if I understand now.

Time passed, and then some more passed, and then even a little more passed. We played tag in the warm summer night. We looked at the stars, we told dirty jokes (I just listened). We'd go "hunting for cats" to terrorize. As I recall, our goal was to find the rarest of all the cat family, the mysterious and haunting "Mexican hairless."

Gary once told me there were Indians in the alley, and I didn't sleep for days. For some strange reason I was terrified they were going to steal our laundry off the clothesline (you know how Indians are).

Peanut butter and jelly sandwiches were consumed by the pound. Kool-Aid was served from plastic Tupperware jugs and canteens under the mimosa tree. Once, when I was following a man with a carriage drawn by a live pony down our street, my bare feet found their way to the doctor's office for my first stitches. We'd get a snow cone at the baseball field next to the swimming pool if we had any money left. All in all, it was pretty damn good; Fat City. We were stylin'. We were nationwide. Then one evening the phone rang in our hallway and there was a loud and violent rip in the seam that held together our tranquility and security. That ring changed everything.

I always tried to get to the phone first, but I couldn't reach it and my stepstool was in the bathroom. I didn't know it at the time but it was the California Highway Patrol. My mother answered the phone.

I remember standing in the hall, her shocked reaction and the seriousness of her voice; her tone as she spoke. I tugged on the hem of her dress, wanting to talk to whomever it was. She ignored me. I tried to listen and watch her reactions. I began to figure out that this was somehow a very important call: more important than the lady across the street Betty Martin, and more important than the insurance man. My mother started to tremble slightly and tears fell from her eyes. She wept softly as she spoke into the receiver. I became frightened and held on to her dress tightly.

She asked questions — questions that scared me. "How bad is he? Is he going to make it?" Her crying got the attention of my older sister Susie. She came into the hallway, drawn from the television set in the living room by my mother's quiet sobbing. She joined my mom by the phone as tears began to swell in her eyes.

"What's wrong?" she asked. "Is Daddy okay?" Susie understood: this was really something bad. I looked at my mother and sister. I didn't know what was wrong or what I could do to stop it.

My mother stared at Susie. "It's Jimmy. He's been hurt in a car wreck," my mom cried.

Streams of tears ran down my sister's face. "Where is he? Is he alright?" she asked.

Kelley began to cry from the other room. This was becoming too much for me. I wanted to go and hide under my bed. I wanted to go into the bathroom and lock the door. I wanted Daddy to come home.

My sister suddenly turned, flew down the hall, and hit the screen door running. I followed after her but she was too fast for me. I stood on the front porch and watched as she ran down the sidewalk in the evening shadows. She dodged two kids on bicycles and never slowed down. She ran past where we weren't supposed to go. I saw her approach a small group of big kids almost in the center of the block. She stopped. Then I watched as she grabbed one of the big kids. After just a moment, they all ran back towards the house. It was Gary, she'd found our big brother Gary. He was big; he would know what to do. Everything would be okay now.

They tore past me and found my poor mother sitting in the hall. I remember this because I had never seen my mother sitting on the floor before.

Gary asked, "What's wrong, Momma? What's wrong with Daddy?" She looked up and told us there had been a terrible car wreck in California and we just had to wait to see if he would be alright. I stood in the doorway of the living room and watched. I didn't want to get too close; *maybe I still don't.*

My dad got better. It took years though, *real* years. He was in the VA hospital in Long Beach for four years. I guess we got used to not having a father, just an occasional voice on the phone that sounded less and less like the man I vaguely remembered. He always called from a payphone, and let it ring just once. That was my mom's signal to call the payphone back. It was cheaper that way.

Once about 1960, the whole family went out to see him. I think it was Father's Day because *The Dallas Morning News* came out and interviewed us. I remember it was a big deal. We went to Love Field airport to fly to California. News crews followed us with microphones and lights and stuff. It was very odd. I asked my mom what was going on with all the people looking at us. She told me we were on TV. I didn't get it. Why would anyone want to watch me on TV? I didn't even have a horse or nothing. Years later, I heard my Uncle Delbert had paid for our trip, I thought it was very a nice thing to do.

By the way, have I mentioned my *very* rich Uncle Delbert? I think he's the most intelligent man I have ever met. He's strong, handsome, a leader of men, and he's got way too much money for his only heir, my cousin Craig. I don't want to start any rumors here, but I heard my cousin Craig might have a bit of a drinking problem (if you know what I mean). You know, a lot of money *could* just be the death of him, could just "push him over the edge," "the straw that broke the camels neck" kinda thing, etc. I think you get the point — enough said.

Anyway, the plane was cool. It was up in the air. I'd never been "up in the air" before. I remember we hit a thunderstorm over West Texas and landed in El Paso to let it pass. The man next to me showed me a "Texas Cigar" he'd bought on his visit to our great state. I swear it was a foot long. He thought it was very funny; I didn't get it.

We landed safely in California. Man, was it something: they had palm trees just like in the movies! Flowers were everywhere. Parts of the airport were not even under a secure roof, so you were still kind of outside. It was open air, like a farmers' market or something. I was really impressed (if that's the right word), because it *did* make an impression on me. It was so different from Texas.

As we were getting our bags, another group of reporters and news people came up to us. They took our pictures and asked us questions. I really wish that I had seen those news stories. Would I have been cute? Would I have been pitiful? "The poor, little boy from Texas who came across the country on Father's Day to see his daddy, more at ten." Oh man, that's too sweet.

I don't know. I don't think I *really* cared. I was probably standin' there with no front teeth and my nose running enough to make you want to vomit. There has never been *anything* "cute" or "sweet" about me as a child. I think my mom was always just being nice to me so I wouldn't find out she was secretly *still* trying to find a doctor who would perform an abortion on me. Even today, every time I see her talking on the phone, I think she's making the arrangements.

The next morning, as we drove to the VA hospital, I saw a bakery with a huge doughnut on top of the building. It was so cool. Everything there was cool. Even the banks were cool: they were made of black lava rock and had large plate glass windows. Also, they had plants growing right inside the building! Banks in Texas *really* looked like the ones from the movie *Bonnie and Clyde*. I even saw a round building there. Now this place California really knew how to live.

The VA hospital had a huge lobby with a marble floor. My mom talked with a nurse at the reception desk while we kids sat down in the corner of the great hall and looked around with mouths agape.

Mom finally came over and told us they had a rule about letting kids upstairs. No one under twelve could go to the patients' ward. My mom had talked the nurse into letting the three eldest kids — Gary, Susie, and me — sneak up one at a time with our mom. I didn't understand, but I remember Susie was very excited.

When it was my turn to go up I followed my mother up on the elevator. We walked through a maze of crowded halls and corridors. All along, there were hideous men smiling and greeting me; men in wheelchairs, men with limbs missing. It scared the hell out of me. I stared at their shocking disfigurement as they smiled and said, "Hello."

My dad was in a wheelchair in the hall outside his room when I first saw him. He smiled. "Give me some sugar." I hugged him the best I could with all the metal and stuff in the way. He reached over and lifted me into his lap. I think we rolled around a little. I think I thought, maybe — it was okay.

Though he got better, my dad was never the same again. He got out of the wheelchair after a time, then walked with the aid of crutches for the next ten years, then without them for the next ten, but he always had a noticeable limp. He's eighty now and pretty much confined to a wheelchair.

We went to visit some cousins the next day. It was my great-grandmother's younger sister's family. They had some cool teenagers and their mom's name was Skeeter. We didn't have any women named Skeeter in Texas.

We had dinner on a patio in a jungle of tropical plants. Bamboo Tiki torches gave the evenings a very wonderful festive atmosphere. The adults had something called "cock-tales" and the air was filled with cool jazzy music, bossa nova, Les Paul, the Everly Brothers, and that commie bastard Harry Belafonte.

We went shopping, it was great — modern, sleek, brightly painted metal, and lots of glass. We were going to the "beach" (whatever that was). I was all for it, just as long as it didn't have legless, smiling men limping around all over the place.

I got a plastic bucket with a shovel and a little powder-blue Scuba-Man on a blister card that came with an assortment of fish. He had an oxygen tank for his back, flippers, a mask, and best of all — a spear gun. It was one of the coolest things I had ever seen. Yeah, let's do this beach thing!

Holy shit!! Did you know that the beach meant the ocean? It's huge, man. There was water everywhere. You couldn't even see the other side. The water rolled and thundered in, crashing in big, swirling waves. They had poured sand all along the edge of the water so you could dig in it and build stuff. Dude, IT HAD AN "UNDER-TOAD!"

I played in the sand and water all day. I was out there havin' fun in that warm California sun; it was wonderful. As it started getting dark my mom and the other women began to gather up all the blankets and picnic gear. It had been the most glorious day of my life: a Coke, some sand, some water, and some toys. What more could I possibly want?

As we were pulling out of the parking space I reached into my new bucket for my Scuba-Man. He was not there. I told my mom and dad he was missing and they made a quick search of the car. My great-aunt was in the next car and she called out through the open window, "What's wrong?"

My mom rolled her eyes and shook her head, "Delbert's lost his Scuba-Man."

My dad got out in the sand on his new aluminum crutches and with the help of our car's headlights he searched the beach for my Scuba-Man. After a while of hobbling around with great difficulty in the deep sand, he gave up and returned to the car. We left and never returned to the beautiful ocean.

2

Sometime in the mid '70s, I started collecting old toys, and in particular toy soldiers. I was wasting time one day strolling through antique shops in Fredericksburg, Texas. In one small shop I noticed three cast-iron World War I doughboy figurines, each about four inches tall. They were painted brown with pink faces and had little blue dots for eyes. Their old-style flat army helmets were painted silver, yet showed a few small spots of rust here and there. I lifted them from their resting place on the display shelf, my hand hefting their weight. They were smooth and rounded and felt comfortable in my palm.

These were the toys of a fifty-year-old man. They were before my time by thirty years. They were foreign to me, these weighty things; foreign to the little boy who still lived inside me. Everything that I had experienced as a kid was made of plastic. I knew there had been a time when earlier generations had played with cast-iron toys, and before that wood. And before that . . . damn, I can't really remember what came before trees. I think it was dirt or something like that. Yeah, it was definitely dirt. I remember now, I'm pretty sure they played with dirt toys before that.

I looked on the bottom of their bases and noted they were marked at $4.75 each. I asked the clerk if she'd take twelve dollars for the lot and she agreed. I figured, I had, without force, successfully gained full command of my first three recruits. I had my own army! I took them to my garage apartment and placed them on a glass shelf. That was over thirty years ago.

Over the next few decades my army of toy soldiers has grown. The more recent acquisitions are the type of "toys" that were very expensive compared to a child's spending limits from 1940-1960; you'd recognize them if you saw them. They were saved for special occasions such as birthdays and Christmas, and given to some lucky little boy in sets of eight. Each, hand painted and packaged in a red windowed box. It was all very formal.

My cousin Craig (the alcoholic/drug addict) is a perfect example of a child raised with the luxury of such beautiful and exotic toys. I remember admiring his rare and expensive possessions on Christmas afternoons, laid out picturesquely on the parlor floor, in their handsome and stylish home. Hand-painted horsemen in bright red tunics rode lead in the front of columns of gleaming, marching soldiers. Silver knights, with colorful plumes atop their helmets stood ready for adventure as the cannon awaited the signal to fire upon the towering castle. Now come on guys, was I crazy? Where the hell did they get this stuff? I never saw anything like this at Valwood Drugs. Where did you find a castle two feet tall?! And why did they choose to keep it hidden from kids like me?

These pretty toys were so foreign to my M.E.Moses/Sears & Roebuck experience, that not only had I never seen such works of art, but I could not even imagine where such things had come from. I began to understand then, that the privileged among us had places and resources unknown to the average or less sophisticated, and I was one of the latter. Let me state however (because it might influence you to have a more favorable opinion of me), I have never been and I am still not jealous or envious of folks with means greater than myself. I stand respectfully in awe of their achievement and wish them only the best, because I knew even back then, that these were my people. This is where I belonged and I hold no disrespect for those unfortunates that have even less than I do (even if they are just a bunch of losers). I know there are those that surpass all on their way to the top of our socioeconomic system through sheer hard work, brains, determination, luck, or a myriad of possibilities or combinations of events or circumstances. And these people can only be stopped by God, or the government.

Somehow, somewhere along the way, I found I had drifted from the theatrical arts (which I had used as a means of support from my teens to my early thirties) into the industrial arts. It seemed like a totally natural move to me. Although, there are those I occasionally meet that find it an unnatural progression.

I learned to paint sets in the theater, now I have a paint shop. I used to play a wooden instrument and sing into a metal microphone on a chrome stand, now I have a wood and machine shop. Nowadays I design and manufacture lighting and furniture, back then I did lighting design and moved furniture. See, it's really the same thing.

Now this just didn't happen overnight and it's not like I'm rolling in money. It took years to build this small company and it's *still* small. And you must also *always* remember: I'm a liar.

One day in the winter of '98 a couple of new clients had me designing and building the interior of a new and exciting family amusement center. "It will be the first of a large chain. It's backed by blah, blah, blah," (I guess I'm not the only liar out there). A lot of my clients have high hopes and must remain extremely optimistic for the sake of the poor bastard that's footing the bill that keeps the gravy train a-runnin'. It's funny, it's like there is absolutely no possibility of failure until (of course) it fails. You should watch the cockroaches scatter in the light. It amazes me every time I see it, and I've seen it many, many times.

Occasionally I ask, "You know folks, are you sure you want to put this much money into something that might not be such a great idea?" However, by the time they get to my level it's usually too late for the financier to bail and he is already in too deep to pull out. So the guy loses his shirt and usually everything else. Friends, if it sounds too good to be true, it usually is. There, at least I tried.

I must admit though, in this *particular* case, they had really thought out their battle plan well. The first flagship-facility was going to be in the entertainment hungry state of California, in the socially neglected and culturally starved city of Long Beach. There was absolutely *no way* this idea could not work.

There, see how easy it is to do? To an idiot that makes sense. So if you liked that last idea, send me your money.

We worked all winter of '98 and spring of '99 on the project. As May approached, my crew made arrangements to leave their wives and families for the installation of the interior package I had designed.

3

About fifteen years ago, I sat in an un-sober state admiring a room full of my toy soldiers. My upstairs library was one of the niches in my house that contained a portion of my collection of antique toys. They were displayed everywhere throughout the house but the library had my favorite concentration of pieces.[1]

I had built my impressive and unique collection up to world-class standing over the years and, I must admit, it was lovely to behold. True, these articles were classic examples of what any collector might aspire to with enough time, money, and luck, but one thing bothered me. I had every toy that any child could ever have dreamt of owning, yet there was something wrong. Something was missing from my collection — they were not really toys any longer. Now they were assets, commodities. They were works of art. They could never be touched by a child again. They had become *too* prized to bring the original pleasure they had been designed for. They were just useless, decorative, delicate little things; just museum pieces really.

That night I decided I wanted even more. I needed something else, I wanted something less, I wanted *my* toys. I needed the healing power of Montgomery Ward. I needed a large kitchen spoon, a pile of sandy loam, and half a dozen Tonkas. I *really* wanted to make roads in my grandmother's garden in the summer sun once again. I wanted to see Zorro, Rin Tin Tin, or Davy, Davy Crockett on the cover of a box on Christmas morning again. I wanted a Texaco Fire Chief Helmet. I wanted a Johnny Reb Cannon. I wanted a gun like

---

[1]Dude, I had a library. Did you catch that? Please note: most dumb-asses do not usually have libraries.

Steve McQueen had in *Wanted: Dead or Alive.* "Where does a person find such things?" I wondered. I had become tired of tax liens, business contracts, and only seeing my kids every other weekend. I wanted my stuff back. I wanted the things that I had loved.

Could I buy back my childhood — or Christmas? Could I locate the things that made me happy? How does a person go about finding such things.

Antique shops, Christie's, and Sotheby's handled all the good stuff as I had learned over the years. But who dealt in crap? Who sold forty-year-old cheap stuff? I intended to find out if there was such a market and what was wrong with the people that supported it. For *these* were truly my people. Thus began my quest for the thing I valued most, my childhood.

I found a small group of people around the country that were sympathetic to my cause. I became a regular on their mailing lists and occasionally I would go to antique toy shows around Texas. I began to slowly acquire the missing pieces of my youth. It was there that I met Ed.

Ed was a full-grown man who loved children's toys. We had many things in common. Ed, like me, would kick your ass if he were in a foul mood. We both enjoyed the Zulu Wars in South Africa, but not just from a military or historical standpoint, we really *liked* 'em. The subject of the Alamo and ancient Rome were also favorites. Ed also smoked cigarettes. What a guy. They don't make them like that anymore, thank God.

Against his will, I forced Ed to come and work for me so we could talk about Hitler and toys and uniforms all day. Ed had been a serious dealer in the toy business in his home state of California before he moved to the Dallas area with his family. Over the time we spent together, Ed tracked down many toys for my collection.

One day I mentioned my Scuba-Man to Ed and he just sat there and nodded. "I know the piece."

A few days later after work we were sitting in my office smoking and talking. Ed pulled a zip-lock baggy from his shirt pocket and tossed it on my desk. It was full of plastic fish. They all had their names on the bases. It was the fish from my lost set. I opened the bag and held them; I remembered them all.

Ed smiled his non-existent smile and laid several minute pieces of plastic next to the fish. It was a small oxygen tank, a set of tiny flippers, a mask, and a spear gun. I looked up hopefully and Ed shook his head. "Sorry, I didn't have any luck with the skin diver."

I looked over the items on my desk, "Wow, thanks man, this is very cool." And it was.

4

As I packed my bags to go to California, my "current" wife and I talked about the trip, my length of stay, and the fact that I was terrified to fly, especially by myself. I'm not going to go into that right now, but I will say this: as a matter of public service, in the heat of summer never, never, NEVER add six thousand pounds of cargo to a full airliner in a desert location, with a *very* short runway, without first informing the captain — enough said.

Anyway, for some strange reason I went to the garage and opened a box marked "Pirates, Scuba, and Aquatic." Inside I found my stored plastic fish and Scuba-Man accessories that Ed had gotten me. I stuffed the bag-o-fish in one of my carry-on bags. I don't know why, but I felt better.

I landed at Long Beach International and was shocked to the point of being speechless as I looked around the small airport. This was the airport from my trip to visit my father forty years before. Nothing had changed, except now I knew a few of the names of the flowers. I stood in disbelief as I discovered the spot where we had talked to the news reporters. The outdoor baggage area was still exactly the same: eerie.

My crew and I worked for several weeks at the project site on Carson Boulevard. Every day on our way to and from the site I would see places I had seen as a child: the bank where my mom cashed a check, the doughnut shops, the restaurants, the cylindrical Holiday Inn tower.

I set my fish on the top of the television set in my hotel room and I explained to them that if I had time we would all take a day off and go to the beach to find our missing Scuba-Man.

The days dragged on and on and I hated the project. I hated everything about the job. My clients sucked. I sucked. And to make matters worse, you couldn't even smoke a cigarette in a bar for Christ's sake! California had gotten weirder than France. I was praying for "The Big One" on an hourly basis. If it took losing me to save the world from this de-evolution, then so be it. I mean really, the California Legislature was actually considering a bill that would repeal the Law of Gravity. They felt it held people down.

One morning I went to the job-site trailer that belonged to the developer to use the fax machine. As the lady in charge was on the phone, I, as always, politely waited. While I stood there I noticed an old, faded blueprint lying on a conference table. In the corner of the print I read the words "Veterans Administration" upside down. I took a step closer and studied the blue lines. They were the blueprints for the Long Beach VA Hospital. There on the front page was the first level, the lobby, where I had sat with my brothers and my sister.

When the lady got off the phone I asked her the relevance of the old print. "Oh, we use that as reference for the old utilities," she replied. I guess she could tell I didn't exactly follow her. She smiled with sudden surprise. "Oh that's right! You're with the group from Texas."

I didn't know at first if she was attempting to be insulting with the "Texas" statement. Was she implying that Texans were ignorant or stupid or barbaric or something? I was within mere moments of drawing the five-shooter I had hidden in my sash, when she walked towards the conference table to join me. She added, "There was an old hospital here for the last sixty years: the Long Beach VA."

I *deja vued*. I *deja vued*. I tilted my head at an angle like a confused dog.

She looked up at me with a questioning face. "You *did* know we built this complex on the old VA hospital site, didn't you?" I shook my head slowly.

She walked over to a large pile of prints and returned with one showing the current project site. She laid it over the old print and used the straight line of Carson Boulevard to line them up. She pointed to the position of the entertainment facility where I had been working the last few weeks. "There's your site," she said and then she lifted the page from the corner while keeping her finger in place. Beneath the new print I saw her finger resting on the corner of the large room I had sat in with my family. I couldn't believe it — I had been working for weeks in what was the lobby of the Long Beach VA Hospital.

Now, I know that you feel that there should be some sort of moral to this tale, I did think seriously about that last night, for a few minutes anyway. It'd be nice if it all fit together without glue and the loose ends were tied up nicely.

I've been described as the most romantic, overly optimistic, generous-to-a-fault man many people have ever met, and I take that as a compliment considering the little shit I've been for so much of my life.

But the best I can seem to come up with is that sometimes we just lose things that mean a great deal to us, and there's nothing that we can really do about it. I don't know why it happens and I don't really think I want to know why.

See, I think that the losses we must endure in life are as important and precious as the soft kisses from our children or our first real love. I think our lives are built of bricks that must contain both drunken bliss and seemingly unbearable sorrow. I think it takes the real pain we suffer to help us grow to appreciate the things that are really important. I don't think I would ever really take to heart the advice of anyone who hasn't felt complete loneliness and helplessness. We are amazing and unbelievably complex entities, ain't we? I, for one, would never want to change anything that might in any way alter the outcome.

5

Okay, okay, I can't stand it: I hate a story that doesn't have a happy ending. I lied, okay, so sue me. Here's what *really* happened:

I finished the job ahead of schedule, and the clients were so pleased with our work that they added a twenty thousand dollar bonus to our last check. I didn't really need the money so I gave it to my devoted men.

My crew took two weeks off and flew to Tahiti to rest while studying the scriptures. I had to go to the Mount Wilson Observatory to clear up some problems they were having with perplexing data that could have potentially meant the end of our universe, or at the very least, several of our local planets.

After that, on my way to the airport, I received a message via a California Highway Patrol helicopter that my assistance was required on the set of a new movie starring Mr. Tom Hanks. I worked one-on-one with Tommy for a few hours, and I think I brought him around.

Finally I relaxed and sipped an ice-cold beer in first class as the plane took off exactly on time. I was delighted to be informed by a beautiful stewardess that the crippled children in coach had seen me board the plane and wanted to meet me. You know me, I could never refuse a child in need.

The beautiful children were of all nationalities and ethnic backgrounds. I loved them all immediately, even the black ones. They were on their way to St. Jude's Hospital for Crippled Children in one of America's most fabulous and scenic cities: Memphis, Tennessee. They were attended by a most caring and thoughtful group of nuns. As I spoke with the children, I found the other passengers drawing near to hear my words, many with moist eyes.

I was overcome with joy and pride as a group of large bikers calling themselves the Widow Makers came forward from the rear of the plane and took a vow to dedicate their lives to the raising of these unfortunate souls.

I was feeling elated that I had been able in some small way to help make a difference in their lives. As I returned to my seat, I had to inform the beautiful stewardess that I was indeed happily married. I think she will get over it and do just fine.

Suddenly there was a tremendous bang and the plane shook violently. The captain called over the intercom for me to come immediately to the cockpit. It was bad. We had lost our space — uhh — rear stabilizer. There wasn't much we could do. I ordered the captain to turn the plane 183 degrees so we would not risk innocent lives on the ground below, *and* I needed time — time to think.

After some quick calculations I realized the odds of landing without mishap were incredibly small. The best I could do was prepare the passengers and crew for the worst and pray for the best.

I decided that our only course of action was a sea landing. The captain gave the controls to me as this was a most hazardous procedure and required a calm and skilled operator. I slid into the control seat as I had so many times before and took charge of the damaged craft.

Frank, the co-pilot, (a man whom I had previously known from my work in Afghanistan for the CIA), turned to me and said, "Okay Big D, show us your stuff."

I grinned and took a cigarette from my breast pocket (that's what professional authors call your shirt pocket). The captain leaned in to light it for me, but I waved him off. "No thanks," I said confidently, "I just quit." Gritting my teeth, I veered hard to port. I now had the craft parallel to the coastline. Below us, I could see the waves rolling silently in slow motion.

Without the use of the vertical stabilizing thingy, I knew it would be tough from a mechanical standpoint to make the plane comply with my demands. I reached into the core of my being and summoned powers I only use on occasions such as this. Because it's a gift from the Creator and is reserved for good works, I use it humbly and sparingly. Not to mention it can cause deep unsightly lines in the area around the eyes, adding years to your appearance. As my physical body reacted to the situation at hand, my spiritual Self became "one-with-all-things." I achieved a higher cosmic plane in which all things are possible. I leaned back and drew in a deep, cleansing breath. I felt the hand of God anoint my head without even messing up my hair . . . and then all things became clear.

Through sheer will alone I forced the plane down. As we descended to the earth below, I gave orders for the crew and passengers to prepare for a bumpy ride. I wanted *all* trays in an upright position and carry-on luggage stowed under the seats or in the storage compartments above.

The moment arrived. There was a sudden jolt as the underbelly of the fuselage kissed the water's surface. I raised the nose slightly in order to reduce the effects of sudden drag. I cut engine speed significantly. As the velocity decreased, I piloted the giant into a controlled and smooth landing. I lowered the nose and I glided the craft to a stop. The nose bobbed only once, slightly, and it was over.

I slapped Frank on the shoulder. "And that," I said quite cleverly, "is how it's done!"

Next, with the aid of the Widow Makers, I organized a group evacuation. I'm happy to say that all the children were delivered safely to the waiting rescue workers on shore.

Once all ninety-one passengers and crew were accounted for I removed my boots, grabbed my carry-on, and dove into the clear, blue water. I swam to the rescue area where the press and onlookers waited, many holding signs praising my efforts. All eyes were on me as I approached from the shallow surf. Before I even reached the security of dry earth the reporters were on me. I was exhausted, but it was hard to refuse the inquiries of my old friend Barbara Walters.

I smiled at Barbara and shook my head: "Give me a minute Barb, would ya?"

My old friend wrapped her arm around my shoulder and helped me onto the beach. "We can talk later, pal," she said, and laid me down in the warm sand. I felt the tension flow slowly from my aching body. My brain began to relax as the events of the day slowly became just another part of my heavily embroidered past. "So, are you going to be alright?" Barbara asked as she stroked my hand softly. I could hear the concern in her timbre.

I paused and took an emotional and mental inventory. I reached my hand into the comforting grains of sand that held my weary body. I held my hand up and let the particles flow like water between my outstretched fingers. As the last of the sand returned to the earth I closed my hand.

It was not until *that moment* that I realized there was something still remaining in my palm. I brought my hand close to my face and raised my head to peer at it. There, once again, my little blue Scuba-Man was held in my loving embrace. I smiled, only slightly, as I turned to my friend. "Yeah, Barb," I finally replied, "I'm gonna be *just* fine."

*This story is dedicated to the memory of my friend
Karl Sloth, who will someday be dead.
Karl, please return my porn first.*

Cara de Mandril

1

I don't know if I've ever told you before but I'm known as the black sheep of my family. Hell, the honest truth is I'm the flatulating, three-legged, pygmy goat of the entire neighborhood (and around the corner up to the house with the broken mailbox). Maybe because of this weirdness, or the arm's distance I've kept from normality, I've always had a morbid special interest in other odd-ball-fucked-up types.

I used to collect these cuddly eccentrics but eventually I ran out of room and had to let them go.

Thanksgiving of '97 I gave thanks that so few cared so little for my particular whereabouts, that I proceeded forth into the mountainous regions of New Mexico.

New Mexico is like a screwed up version of California, if you can grasp such a concept. The people are mixed in their culture in odd and even ways. You see Native Americans that are black with blue or green eyes, and burned-out, caustic "mountain mammas" with wide, robust hips and skin as weathered and cracked as the dry cliffs. There's a large lesbian population and *not one of them* is the kind you see in the movies. Smatterings of national and international celebrities are distributed frugally over the landscape, but just enough for you to say sarcastically, "Wow, really? Who? Oh yeah, you gettin' hungry yet?" What's *really* cool is when the celebrities are also one of the lesbians, but you're not supposed to know it. So, you know, be cool dude.

There are itsy-bitsy, little-bitty cowboys standing in three-hundred-year-old bars with moustaches and hats so big that you can actually see them on the local maps. It's the newest New Age, the upgraded version 7.5; the *real* New Age. Hey, I've got your New Age right here, buddy. It's calibrated to an atomic clock daily to ensure freshness.

Crystal worshipers, nudists, magnetists, they're all in this big pen that surrounds the state for easy viewing. This is the dreamland of Oppenheimer, the backdrop for Billy the Kid and Georgia O'Keeffe. Oh yeah, and let's not forget about those mutant defenders of Mother Earth in Roswell. There are farmers, ranchers, cultists, and microchip engineers all drinking from the same infected trough. Needless to say, I fit right in.

I arrived in Santa Fe in the early evening and went to the Inn and Spa at Loretto just off the square. The Inn is one of those beautiful adobe structures with lots of tile and rough timber. Despite its Old World architecture, it's got all the good stuff an asshole like me requires.

I sat in the bar and talked with the bartender for a few minutes. The large fireplace glowed and radiated warmth I felt across the grand room. The pinyon wood filled my normally comatose nostrils with its pungent fullness. Old Navajo textiles and paintings using the gouache hues of teal and burnt orange hung about the large stucco cavern.

Yeah, it was nice and quaint and the bartender was an absolute knockout. I'm sure she was being so nice to me because I was a hunk, and not because I was throwing my money around like a drunken Texan. Alas, I needed sustenance so I strolled through the expanse of corridors until I found a quiet restaurant tucked down one of the hallways.

I had cold turkey with stale dressing and a good bottle of wine, and I was happy. I didn't complain, because the way I figure it, I should have been dead years ago anyway. So this was like, you know, free.[1]

So I stumbled back to the bar and plopped my worthless carcass down on a barstool. I drank and talked with the bartender some, and listened to the music playing on the

---

[1]Did I mention the church? I'm sure I did, but you probably weren't listening.[2] There's a church in the hotel. More exactly, they built the hotel around an old church or something like that. Get the picture? It's a lovely stone chapel with miniature everything in it: little doors, little windows, little statues of God and stuff for a little congregation. It was built by the Sisters of Loretto, perhaps you've heard of them? I think they were German. It was built in the nineteenth century. I think, and you might have actually seen it on *The World's Most Unsolvable Mysteries* or *Nova: the Unseen World of Staircases* or something like that. As the legend goes, the nuns (or Nuns? I'm not sure) had very little money. So they built this tiny church as if it were a jewel box; one would actually have trouble shooting a game of pool there on a regulation size table ... trust me on this one. I know what I'm talking about.

So it's small, get it? So small that they couldn't put in a staircase and the choir couldn't get to the choir loft on Sunday mornings (or whenever Catholics worship whatever it is they worship) without the aid of a ladder. After about a century of this royal pain in the ass, the good "sistas" decided it was time to pray to God (or whomever they pray to) for some relief from this obvious liability.[3] When you combine this with the fact that Germans just

speakers that were placed around the lounge. There were only a few people sitting in the dim, flickering light talking and laughing. Yet even with the background music, it was quiet. Every now and then a small burning ember would be ejected from the fire.

On the far end of the large room, out on the darkened dance floor, I noticed the backside of a large hulking creature. From my vantage point I couldn't tell if he was out there on the dance floor all alone. He had wide, rotundly massive shoulders that appeared deformed as they drooped forward like a hunchback's. His feet were mammoth and slow. Their sheer mass required only a modest exertion from gravity. His neck was nothing more than a chest in the wrong place. From his silhouette I could see his left hand as it rose and fell in three-quarter time to the soft music. He stepped in a lumbering, reserved gait that seemed unusual and out of place at first, yet there was an odd grace in his movements. It wasn't just inexperience alone: he moved as if he was — oh, what's a good word for it — afraid? It was as if this unnatural act of rhythm were so foreign to his regimen that his body overcompensated for its traditional cumbersome clumsiness. He was stiff, but despite all the adjustments and calibrations, it came

---

have to sing, God (in his infinite wisdom and stuff) looked down and sent this little man with his burro to help them (you ever tried to stop a German from singing?).[4]

So this little dude looked around the church and scratched his ass. "Hey, there really *is* no place to put a staircase in here. Why'd y'all do this? Hey God," he said, "check this out."

The little guy thought and thought, and I think I heard somewhere, maybe on *Nova*, that he also drank a beer. He sat there on his ass and drank a beer and tried to figure a way to put a staircase in this tight, cramped space.

Finally, God got bored and sent him a text. "Yo, you're embarrassing me here dude, make like, you know, what do I call those things? Oh right, a 'circular staircase.' Yeah, that's it, a 'circular staircase.' Put it over there in the corner where the confessional is — like these people have anything to confess." The little guy got off his ass and went to work.

out just about right. It was a forced grace, true, but it was in its own way graceful.

He turned like a soft breeze on an August night, holding his left hand rigid and supine with large fat fingers held tightly together and pointing outward. As he came about on the dance floor, for the first time from beneath his lumbering, behemoth form, I glimpsed a tiny woman.

She was a lovely image to behold. With her pale skin, large dark eyes and short raven hair, she looked like a fairy flitting about this towering beast. She looked up at his face and smiled. Her rose cheeks were soft and her eyes sparkled. Her skin was as smooth and flawless as a still mountain lake. I could see them talking softly together as they held each other, this crumbling granite mountain and this delicate crystal. I could also tell that they were new to one another in the way they easily smiled as the other spoke.

I turned back to the bartender to see if any of this was registering as unique, but she was miles away.

Was I the only one who saw this? Was this commonplace?

The man eventually turned around and I saw his face for the first time. It was nothing short of hideous. I feel bad about saying this but it's the truth. His face was long and his jaw hung there like a punching bag, his mouth agape like someone about to sneeze. You could see his tongue lying quietly and bloated in its moist cage. He had blond-red hair so fair that it appeared as if he had no eyebrows. His skin

---

I'm sure the dude was cool and all, but he must have been slower than, oh hell, I don't know, something slow like a turtle or a sloth, 'cause it took him a long time, but it was worth it.

It really is an amazing thing to behold. It does two complete 360s, has NO CENTER SUPPORT, no handrail, and no vertical supports; it just hovers. I've heard that it has no nails in it. It really does just kinda float.

2... as usual, and while we're at it, when's the last time you flossed?

3 Remember the litigious twentieth century was approaching, and have I mentioned yet just how much I HATE lawyers?

4 Man, I'm telling you it's like tryin' to take a banjo away from an Eskimo. Once again, you just gotta trust me.

was white, almost on the verge of being transparent. He was easily, hands down, the Ugliest Man in the World.

This is the kinda stuff I live for, sitting here watching and waiting. I couldn't believe my eyes as I watched them. She was not only unafraid of this grotesque animal, but I think she really liked him. I don't know if she was seeing the same man I was seeing. I think it was actually a lot worse than that — I think they loved each other. I think I knew that they loved each other before *they* knew. I had witnessed two people falling in love. That was the exact moment they fell in love. I could tell. I'd never really seen it before, but I knew. This was love.

2

My friend Cliff (whom I've know through music for decades) has a mountain cabin in Green Mountain Falls, just outside of Colorado Springs. In Dallas, we'd been talking about going up there for at least twenty years. Finally, in the summer of 2001, we made it.

Peabody, the most emotionally dead person I've ever had the pleasure to meet, went with us. Peabody and I never got along entirely well. See, Peabody had a strong suspicion that I was an idiot, but had no hard proof — whereas I *knew for a fact* that he was a moron. This guy could bring down the heavens. He is arrogant, distant, and a completely hollow shell of a man. It was like looking in a mirror.

Anywho, we drove up and then got down. There was an abundance o-sittin', and lots of lookin'. It was scenic and quiet. Perhaps it was a bit too primitive for my taste. I hung with my usual flair and didn't kill anybody, or needlessly spill innocent blood over our living conditions.

One day we drove up to Gypsum and saw some

---

[5]Do you think I've pissed off enough people yet?

musician friends of ours that were playing at an outdoor venue. It was on the other side of the state and took several hours at high speeds to get there. Being from Texas though, a drive across a little pussy state like Colorado is as easy as shooting a cat. I don't think I'll ever understand why people from Colorado don't like Texans. I don't know, maybe they're just jealous 'cause we don't have all those mountains to mess with or maybe it's just because they have such small penises.[5]

Friends, I'm sorry to report that Gypsum got gypped. It was like only *this* far from Vail, but those few miles make all the difference in the world. It's right there off the highway just like Vail, except it sucks even worse.

Just before you enter the area around Gypsum, the land and the foliage drops off to an Oklahoma or West Texas standard drab. The people there were actually quite nice, but I didn't feel like that alone was quite enough to put 'em over the top with the Travel Channel. Gypsumites, hear my words: verily you might want to get some comfortable kneepads. Hey, don't blame me for your forefathers' lack of business sense.

So Cliff, Peabody, and I hung around all day at the "Gypfest." The event was held on the town green and all the locals were there. I felt sympathy for the townspeople's plight and plot, so I had a beer a little earlier than usual (I'm still having a little trouble getting over it, even today).

We watched some national Nashville country music acts, which I just loathed. It was nothing but high-tech pop music with a dim-witted southern drawl glued on. Oh Nashville, brothers, why do you want country groups to sound like the Bee Gees?

Due to the festival, there were absolutely no rooms to be had in Colorado from Grand Junction to Denver. There was loose talk among our friends of free rooms at the Ramada after the band checked out at midnight, or one o'clock, or two o'clock at the most. Cliff and Peabody wanted to hang loose and score one of these free rooms.

So, after the concert, we met our friends, the other musicians, and the road crew at a little poolhall in town. Everybody was wound up, ready to relax and party, but I found myself to be lacking in sobriety and snap. I was therefore dragging ass both publicly and privately, about to collapse from alcohol poisoning and a lack of proper nourishment. Having no choice in the matter, I took a seat and tried to act awake.

"So, ah, what time do you think you guys will be pulling out?" I asked the guitarist nonchalantly. "Man," I mumbled, shaking my head with evil intent, "it's a long drive to Omaha. I'm sure glad it's not me. Have you ever seen the women in Omaha? You look tired, you feeling okay?" But nothing seemed to push them. So I continued to wait for a free room soiled by a musician on the road. Whoopee.

Somewhere around three in the morning I walked to the parking lot, got in my car and started driving towards Denver, leaving Cliff and Peabody behind. I remember giggling like a twelve-year-old girl as I slid down the interstate watching the mile markers fly by in the darkness. The road was extremely smooth and devoid of other night crawlers, so I was propelled forward at an amazing rate of speed. After just a few clicks, I managed to make it to some obscure exit where I saw a few friendly lights in the distance. There I found a great little hotel and crashed like — oh, I don't know, I just crashed, okay (sorry, I haven't eaten all day).

In the morning I kinda realized I had left Peabody and Cliff in the bar somewhere out there in the barren wasteland that is western Colorado. I called Peabody's cellphone and told him I was in this little town forty miles away and about to enjoy room service. We agreed we'd meet in a short while at my hotel.

Peabody explained he could get a ride from some lady banker he'd met the night before. An hour later, I watched him as he stumbled out of her car and into the gas station that was in the parking lot of my hotel. Man, he looked like fried shit in a nice vomit sauce. I was thrilled.

"So what time did they leave?" I asked.

"I dunno, four-thirty — five," he said.

I smiled.

In the line to pay for our merchandise Peabody looked at me and asked, "Is Cliff ready?"

I laughed. "Yeah right."I thought for a minute and then turned back to Peabody. "What do you mean exactly?"

Peabody looked at me like I was even crazier or something. "You seen Cliff yet this morning?"

"No," I answered and again there was a pause, "why?"

Peabody shrugged his shoulders. "Just wonderin."

Something didn't feel right. "Pea-brain," I moaned, "but *you've* seen Cliff today, right?"

Peabody looked up, befuddled. "No, I thought he left last night with you."

Well, as you remember, he didn't (see previous page) and it took us half a day to find him without the aid of a cellphone. It turned out that Cliff had been back in Gypsum, sitting like a dumb-ass in the lobby of the Ramada, waiting for Peabody to wake up.

One bright point was that Peabody puked all the way back to Green Mountain Falls, and I think he might have had a problem with his bowels (not really, but this is my story). Once there, we spent a few days recuperating and then Peabody caught a ride back to Dallas with the lady banker (who later wanted to become a Dixie Chick and then decided not to when she found out you needed talent, like nunchuck skills). I was genuinely sorry to see them go, as I had accidently left my smokes in her car.

A day or two later, Cliff and I left Colorado and headed down to Taos, New Mexico, to shoot some footage of another band playing a gig down there.

Now Taos is a cheaper version of Santa Fe. Most of the smug waiters and waitresses that belittle you in Santa Fe actually live over the mountains in Taos. They get their coffee from 7-Elevens and most of them are from normal places like Kansas or Indiana. If you have a watch that works they think you're showing off. The people from Santa Fe have way too much money to worry about, or rub elbows with, trash like you and me.

My friend Mike was the lead singer of the band we were videotaping in Taos. We had been friends since grade school in Texas. Cliff and I stayed at the Sagebrush Inn, which is a place I swore I'd never visit again. The Sagebrush is cool to look at, but it's full of, well you know, people from Taos.

The Sagebrush is the ONLY restaurant in the world where I actually had to walk into the kitchen to find somebody who could bring me the rest of my meal. The witless waitress set a steak on the table and just left: no drink, no silverware, nothin'. The "chef" was leaning against a prep table smoking, talking with my waitress, when I stormed in. They were amazed at my audacity. They just stood there staring at me. I guessed most of their clientele were way too stoned to be able to walk that far.

I said, "Excuse me, can I please have our side orders, something to drink, and some silverware? It's been twenty minutes!"

The road-weary bitch rolled her eyes, took a drag off her cigarette and said, "Sir, guests are not allowed in the kitchen." What an absolutely worthless piece of shit (we've been happily married for fifteen years).

Well anyway, here I was back at the Sagebrush, hoping the staff didn't remember me. We left the hotel that afternoon to meet Mike and the band. They were playing at a nice little civic center up in the hills above Taos. Cliff and I set up the equipment and got some shots of the guys as they came in.

We were using Cliff's camera. He was doing this as a

favor to me for twenty years of me pickin' up the bar tab and one broken windshield. I had gotten a quote from Scorsese for about half of that amount.

"Well, I guess this makes us about even," Cliff said as he began taping.

Now let me get this straight, I pay every food and drink tab, every hotel bill for twenty years — he puts a camera on his shoulder, pushes a button, and we're even? Hey Cliff, what about my windshield?

The band looked and sounded great. The existing lighting in the hall was good. The selected song had already been recorded, so we taped several versions of them lip-syncing to it as the crowd began to arrive. When the band began to play we got lots of footage of each member to use as incidental shots. The plan was to do the song live once at the beginning of the night and once more towards the end. Everything was working pretty well.

One thing that I really love about this part of the world is its dancing. Now, I think that anyone who knows me can tell you I'm not a dancin' kinda guy, but this place is something else. There's no place like it on Earth. They have the most unique, inspired way of expressing themselves. It's happy. It's romantic. They dance as if living were a celebration. Hey, it's *so* good, even I like it. As much as I bitch about things, I must say this to you: before you die you really should do yourself a favor and go to New Mexico and watch the dancers — just don't stay at the Sagebrush.

During the show I had to shove Cliff around here and there in hopes that he'd push that damn magic button every now and then with the camera pointing at something worth capturing.

In the middle of the first set, Cliff was lying on the floor videotaping people's feet while they danced. He shot the couples as they twirled and pranced about.

I stood over in a corner, nursing a beer, watching for

interesting people when I saw the Ugliest Man in the World on the far side of the room. I watched him step from the darkness into the light of the dance floor. It was him. It was the guy from years before and the beautiful little woman was accompanying him. For a moment my mean 'ol heart smiled.

As the music played, they began to move and sway in the same graceful, staccato flow I remembered from the night in Santa Fe, but they had improved greatly. The couple now showed more flare, more confidence, more refinement. I took a big chug-o-my-beer and leaned against the wall and just watched. I was happy to see them. You know, for a registered jerk (in good standing), sometimes things can even get to me. You know what I mean?

I had Cliff shoot them, but I didn't really think we'd be able to use it because, well, the guy was *really* ugly.

Later in the night, Mike was taking a really hot solo on his guitar and walked to the edge of the stage like he was Mitch Jaggar. He was gettin' down and the people standing on the floor in front of the stage were cheering him on and watching his fingers as they flew up and down the fretboard. There in the middle of the crowd was Ugly Guy standing calmly as the others around him moved rhythmically to the music. I saw Mike's face brighten for a second and then a smile broke out. The Ugly Guy held a little boy up towards my friend Mike as he played. The little boy was holding a miniature guitar!

The little boy strummed energetically, trying to keep pace with Mike. Ugly Guy held the toddler mere inches away from Mike's guitar. The kid mimicked Mike's every move. They were jammin'!

Mike began laughing. The band laughed, the audience loved it. I was digging it, and Cliff — and Cliff had gone for a beer.

So we missed it — we missed it.

So what, ya know? So fuckin' what? Who really cares anyway? Some ugly guy holding up some ugly little kid — big fucking deal, I got to see it though and that was kinda nice.

We finished up the night and Mike and I shot the breeze as we packed up our gear. I told Mike the story of the father of the little boy with the miniature guitar.

"Oh, that's Cara de Mandril," Mike said with a grin.

I stopped. "Caradine who?"

Mike laughed. "Cara de Mandril," he whispered, "Baboon Face, that's what the Mexicans call him, but I think he looks more like an orangutan."

"Oh," I said and rolled up an extension cord.

I thought for a moment, then muttered, mostly to myself I suppose, "The bit with the kid and the guitar was funny."

Mike looked up, smiled and nodded. "Yeah, I liked that. The kid always loves to hear us play." He threw some power cords in a big trunk and picked up his beer off an amplifier. He tilted his head back and took a drink, and I watched him look at the ceiling for a long time. When the beer disappeared, Mike wiped his mouth and looked at the floor in thought.

"The little guy has had a lot of problems," Mike said softly. "You know, health problems. It's been rough on him. And it's really been rough on his parents, too."

I nodded my head.

"I don't know if they're gonna make it, ya know?" Mike continued, "I've heard rumors about them splitting up." He shrugged his shoulders. "It's too bad. They were a nice couple."

The next morning I got in my car and drove home. I haven't talked to Cliff much since we finished the video, but that's not unusual. Sometimes we go years even when we're sitting next to each other at the bar.

Peabody did the editing on the video and it came out wonderful. The asshole really did a great job. I've seen it a hundred times or more. It's a work of art.

I think the music is the best piece that Mike has ever written. He wrote it with a guy named Shake and I love it every time I hear it. The images of the dancers and the score blended together perfectly and I wouldn't have changed a single frame, which is highly unusual for me.

To shut me up during the editing, Peabody put in a few seconds of the couple for me. They're a little obscured, so they're just fine. Nobody even notices them but me.

I don't know whatever became of them or the little boy. I hope he's a big boy now, but life can be brutal.

Sometimes I sit with Comet on the front porch and think about my life and what it would be like if I had made different choices. Sometimes I get feeling a little sad. Sometimes I feel sorry for that couple, but usually I think I feel sorry for myself.

AN OPEN LETTER TO STEVEN SPIELBERG

It was a Friday. I had just finished up another incredibly average week of tedious busywork. It had been a week of hopeful expectation and wasted optimism. There had been precious few truly relaxed moments of accomplishment and satisfaction. I hate it when it's like that. The business climate is stagnating: every day there's another tale of woe that some billion dollar conglomerate forgot to move the decimal point on their annual return, or *meant* to add a "minus sign" before their bottom line.

"Oops," the CEO says to one of the reporters, "we meant we *lost* 3.8 billion. My mistake." Then he'll pause for a millisecond with a weird expression carved on his face. He'll open his mouth slightly but nothing comes out. A man in an expensive suit leans over and whispers in his ear.

"Perhaps I should rephrase that," the CEO says with a nervous smile and a stutter. "The *corporation* lost 3.8 billion. It's the CFO's mistake. I was so busy selling my stock that I didn't have time — oops." Cue the guy in the suit.

So you probably get the picture. I'm not trying to be negative and I hope your business is okay, and that your family and friends are healthy and fruitful, but I'm sure everybody realizes it's a little tough out there right now. It'll get better, so just try to be happy and hang on.

I like it when I'm slammed and there are lots of orders.[1] Then everybody is busy and has enough to make ends meet. I guess we all do.

So it was six o'clock, or thereabouts, and I was futzing around really doing nothing in an attempt to feel useful when the phone rang. It was my (current) wife (at the time).

"When are you coming home?" she asked in a way that told me she was hungry, yet had no intentions of making dinner.

"I don't know, why?" I responded.

"Oh, I don't know, just wondering."

I could tell it had been the same kinda week for her. She was bored.

"I don't want to come home," I said. "Let's go get a drink or something."

To my surprise, she perked right up. "Ooo-kay."

We met at a little bar near our home. It's really close, but the people are so old there it's almost funny. Almost.

There was no place at the bar, so we stood and talked

---

[1] I just did a typo and it read, "I like it when there are lots of odors."

with the old farts. We politely waited our turn to top their conversations. I had all my barroom banter and jokes neatly arrayed in order and ready for use.[2] I guess I kinda feel like I owe the poor old things a little laughter and sunshine in their waning years, it's the least I can do. After all, they did kill Hitler for me.

One nice thing about this bar, though, is that due to the average age of the clientele, you really never have to wait very long for a seat at the bar. Normally if you wait a few minutes one of them usually dies, or has to go to the bathroom, and thus vacates their seat.

"Sorry, Gramps," I laugh in my mind cleverly, "you snooze, you lose. Now you just stand there and finish your drink while Grandma and I take care of business — if you know what I mean. You got a problem with that?"

So anyway, my wife and I are standing there feeling all "youthful and attractive." I looked around at the sad state of affairs I had led myself into. "I've got to do something with my life," I moaned. "I'm dyin' here."

Patti looked at me in her understanding way. "What do you mean?"

I shook my head. "I dunno exactly. I just *need* something. *Something more.*" I paused and thought (but not deeply). "I've wasted my life. I've accomplished nothing."

"What do you want to do?" she asked.

"You know, have money, power, respect, that kinda stuff," I answered.

"Well, why don't you do *something* then?" she countered.

I chuckled at her naiveté. "Patti," I began, "it's *not* quite that simple. I'm just a normal guy in many ways; I'm not really all *that* special. Just like everyone else, I put my pants on one leg." Then, like a wink from a transsexual, it hit me. Maybe she was right — again.

---

[2]When I ran spellcheck, the computer kicked out the word "jokes" and insisted that it should read "joke." Man, does this box know me or what!

40

I really needed to do *something*. It was as simple as that. "Patti, what can I do?"

"Why don't you send off some of your writings to a publisher?" she asked.

"Yeah, that's it," I said as it slowly dripped in. I could be one of those famous writer guys. I could get rich and move to California and start doing cocaine. I'd have lots of hot babes and stuff. It'll be great. I would hang with all the big dogs and laugh at all you little guys. Man, I can hardly wait!

"Okay, okay," I said excitedly, "I'll send some stuff off to *Playboy* and *The New Yorker* and all the other top publications. I know they'd just love me!" I can't believe I hadn't thought of this before. "You think they can get the money here before next Friday?"

"Why don't you start off a little more realistically?" she cautioned.

Well, I wasn't about to be stopped now, not now, not by some barfly, not after so much of my life had gone into this: all my hopes and dreams, all my sacrifices.

"Hey, don't you try and hold me back. I could buy and sell you *and* your lame opinions. Let's remember who holds all the aces around here." (Oh, I'm just gonna love this power thing.)

"You could write an article for one of those airplane magazines," she said. "You know, the ones in the pocket in front of you on the plane. They always have interesting articles in there."

I laughed and touched her cheek, remembering the carpal tongue syndrome she occasionally suffered from. "Honey, I'm way too good for that." The poor misguided girl didn't have a clue about the way things really worked in this business. "Besides," I explained in that caring way that I have, "they only pay like, you know, ten or twenty dollars a word or something ridiculous like that."

I could tell she was pondering my words and I think she

was just on the verge of comprehension when she blurted out over the straw in her White Russian, "They're captive, ya know?"

"Honey, who's captive?"

"The people on the plane, they *have* to be there." She stared at me. "For hours sometimes. They just have to sit there and look for something to do." She was ranting and I tried to reason with her.

"Patti," I said slowly and softly, "people on planes don't spend money for those things, they're free. Besides," I continued, "people who fly on planes are stupid. You know that."[3]

She just wouldn't stop. Sometimes she can be so hardheaded. I had to act like I was listening to her. I even nodded my head a couple of times to make it look convincing, like I cared. Man, when I get to California she'll be so gone.

"You know, even Steven Spielberg has to sit there and wait just like everybody else ..." I heard her mumble.

"What?" I asked. "What did you say about Steven Spielberg?"

She stopped. "Oh, I mean, you know, even he has to sit there, too."

"Why's he sittin' there? He's Steven Spielberg! HE doesn't have to do anything he doesn't want to," I said.

"Uh-huh, he sits there bored just like everybody else."

"Wow, I had never thought of that." I was intrigued. "So Patti, tell me more about this dream of yours. Why would Mr. Spielberg be up in the sky sitting there all bored and stuff?"

She sucked on her straw. "He's going to New York to get scripts and stuff and I've heard that he always carries around this big, old steamer trunk full of money to give to the guys who write his movies and stuff." She thought

---

[3]Note to Editor: Make SURE we change this before publication. It could be misconstrued as "harsh," even though we all know it's true.

some more. "Then he gets ANOTHER trunk full of money and he takes all the guys from New York back to California to be rich and famous. They all sit in first class and drink champagne and talk about their next big movie deal. And do you know what?"

I shook my head. That's what I do sometimes when I don't "know what."

"They have a big problem," she said touching my drinking hand.

"They do?" I queried quietly so no one else could hear.

She shook her head. "They don't have a script."

"Wow," I said dumbfounded, "they don't have a script?"

"And then one of the guys says, 'Hey Spiely, have you seen this article in the airplane magazine?' And Steven Spielberg says to him, 'No, I haven't. Don't those things cost money?'"

"And the other guy rises from his seat with the magazine and a bottle of champagne and walks to Mr. Spielberg and hands him the magazine and says, 'Yes, they cost a lot of money, but you can have my copy to keep.'"

"And guess what?" Patti prompted, holding her breath.

"What?" I returned, not wanting to be left behind.

"It's your article!" She laughed. "It's your story that Steven Spielberg has to make his new movie about. They have to, they've got no choice — they've got no script."

Wow! This is SO cool: my story, a major motion picture show by Mr. Steven Spielberg. I couldn't believe I hadn't already exploited the shit outta this. I nodded my head. I now had a direction. I now had a director. I now had a purpose in life — so that's why I'm writing this.

I'd appreciate, in advance, any help that *you* could possibly give me. You know, like, if you see Steven Spielberg on the plane and he's not reading the magazine or something like that. Oh yeah, if you're one of those guys who fly around with him and all that money, be sure and tell him about what we're trying to do here. I'll make it worth your while, if you know what I mean.

Hey, while we're at it, I'll just go ahead and make this all "official" and "legal." Anyone who gets one of my stories made into a film by Mr. Steven Spielberg can expect a reward of $200 (cash). If you don't believe this offer is for real, send me a picture of Steven Spielberg's empty, wanting hands, and I will respond with a photo of the cash.

In closing, I'd like to thank all the little people that helped to make this crazy journey we call life so rewarding for me. We'll get together soon, I promise. But I'm warning you right now, don't get uppity with me, 'cause I can break you like a toothpick.

And last, but not least, I'd like to thank Mr. Steven Spielberg for all the things he's going to do for me and all the fond memories we're going to experience together in the future. I love you all.

Oh yeah, one more thing I just thought of. You know that old hag that sits at the bar every night, Pat or Patsy or whatever her stupid name is? What's *her* deal? Man, you think *you* got problems. Jeez, she just sits there day in, day out, saying the same old crap *over* and *over*. I just hate walking in and seeing the only seat available at the bar is next to her. Her face looks just like a piece of chewed up gum — with hair in it!

"I don't believe we've met" she says, EVERY SINGLE TIME I sit anywhere near her. She bats her crusty old eyes and says, "My name is Pat or Patsy or whatever." I usually just smile and nod back at her. It never fails, she always begins rambling, no matter how far away she is or how loud the music might be.

"I'm Irish," she says every few minutes. "I was born and raised in Dublin, Ireland." And then she sits there on her old drunken, flabby ass and stares at you until you respond. What are you supposed to say? "Wow! Dublin? That's amazing! Tell me all about it."

Steve, what is it about me that makes people think I care? Man, I swear to you Stevie, one of these nights I'm going to turn to that old broad and say (loud enough for everyone at the bar to hear), "You know lady, you say the same thing every time I see you. You're always so drunk you never even remember having told me all this stale crap just last night." She'll stare at me in shocked horror and disbelief. It'll be great!

"Now you just need to go on ahead and give up the ghost," I'll tell her, "and get it over with for your own sake. You're taking up valuable room at the bar." It'll be so cool.

Stevie, I'm telling you right now, that between her and me, one of us is not going to make it. Either she goes, or I go. You know what I mean? It's like, one of us is going to die over this, you know?

Man, I can see it now. We'd walk in, you and me, and I'd tell her off. She'd grab her purse so quick and then call for her tab, sobbing and blubbering. She'd move like she hadn't moved in years.

You know, I don't want to be mean or cruel, but somebody has just *got* to kill her. You know?

You know what's really bad though? Even if we were to tell her off, once and for all, and she started crying, "You cruel bastards, I'm moving back to Dublin," it wouldn't really matter. The truth is, tomorrow night, she'll walk right back in, sit down, turn to me, and say, "I don't believe we've met."

Steve-o, man, I mean it, let's do this thing. Call me.

SPECTATING

Sometimes I feel like I owe you guys some kind of explanation — or excuse — for the things I write about, or why I say what I say in the way I say it. Trust me, my life, thoughts, and lies are used as cheap fodder for our mutual amusement.

I mean, shit, where should I begin? Oh, how's this for a start: MY NAME IS DELBERT!

You try giving it a spin sometime, big man. That's right, just put it on, walk around in it for about ten years, and see if you don't end up in prison. My family would be at Woolworth's or some place when I was a kid, and one of my brothers would say, "Hey Delbert!" But I wouldn't turn around out of sheer embarrassment. In the first grade, my pretty, new teacher called roll on the first day. "Pullen, Delbert," and then she looked around the large cinderblock room. Some of the kids laughed. I just sat there. She tried again, "Delbert, are you here?" I slowly raised my hand. She smiled sweetly. "So, you're Delbert?"

I nodded my head a little in agreement.

"What do your friends call you?" she asked.

"What do you mean?" I questioned.

She smiled again. "You know, at home. What do they call you?"

I looked at the other kids and then the teacher. I whispered, "Delbert."

A strange look came over her face and she shook her head in pity. "Hmm," she grunted.

Let's see, what else? Oh yeah, I graduated high school 525 in a class of eight hundred. All my friends went to college and graduated. I went to college and drank. Graduating never once entered my mind.

I played music from the age of fourteen until thirty and I wasn't all that bad. It was a lot of fun and definitely had its perks, but it was also the hardest I've ever worked. I wouldn't recommend it as a lifestyle for the faint of heart — or if you're ugly.

Okay, what else? Oh, I have a fear of crowds, but I can do it if I have to. I don't normally like new places, but I can do that, too. I don't like airplanes anymore, but I have a really good reason for that one. I have little truck with shy people. I've been known to be a jerk at times, but I've learned that's okay — at times. I feel nauseous when I hear the theme song from *I Love Lucy*. I'm not really much of a cat person, but I don't hate them either, I forgive them. I don't like telling the whole truth. The one thing I hope nobody ever finds out about me is the fact that sometimes my socks don't match inside my boots. And I really don't mind dumb people being around me as long as they wash up first.

I like kids and old people. I have a terrible memory. I like New Orleans and Amsterdam. I hate Paris so far. I think if I had lived a former life, I would have been just as boring

47

and useless as I am now. The person most like me in great literature would have to be Bob Cratchit. The best rock song ever written is "The Mayor of Simpleton." I like Doc Watson and Tom Waits. I hate Tom Brokaw, Peter Jennings, and Dan Rather. I think Dan might be redeemable. He seems honest and objective, doesn't he? I have a deep-seated and lifelong dread of running out of mustard. In my mind I see myself dressed up like Kirk Douglas — okay, okay, Tony Curtis in *Spartacus* — opening up the kitchen cupboard to find it completely barren and void of all French's products. I can't believe we let Patsy Cline live long enough to sing those wretched songs before we finally took the bitch out.

I sometimes sit and wonder for no good reason where all the Stuckey's stores went to (I think they're most likely in Argentina or Peru), and why ALL the 7-Elevens are on the OTHER side of the street. Oh, and I've got a terrible memory … so now, maybe you see what we're up against here. What we've got to work with.

All in all, I've got few regrets. Sure, like most people I wish I had done more with the time I've wasted. I wish I'd drank more, bitched more, slept a little less, and masturbated more.

Anyway, I wanted to tell you about last weekend, which because of my winded introduction is not even "last weekend" anymore, and it won't ever be again.

I know it might seem otherwise, but I don't really get to take a lot of vacations. I do tend to make the most of the ones I get, and I always manage to keep a little something from everyplace I've ever been. Sometimes it's weird, but there's always a small souvenir, some seemingly insignificant tiny knick-knack sitting on a dusty shelf in my cluttered attic just waiting to be picked up and looked at.

Sometimes in the summer, we'd get to go to Valwood swimming pool. I always loved going to the pool. It was wonderful. I remember seeing the sign that hung on the back wall in the booth where you paid to get in. It was hand-painted with black letters on a white glossy background. It was stuck up on a light green wall where all the cool lifeguards hung out with their transistor radios, their silver whistles, and that white stuff on their cool noses. The sign read: Swimmers $.25, Spectators $.10.

I asked my sister Susie what the words meant, and she told me what the sign said. I asked her what a "spectator" was. She told me it was "someone that just watches." I nodded my stupid little head as that concept sunk in. Some people didn't *get* to swim.

We'd swim all day long and then my sister and I would walk back home as the tired, orange sun sank into the field behind the shopping center. It was a pretty long way back home but I didn't care.[1]

Anyway, what I wanted to tell you — where was I? Oh yeah, my wife's sister Paula and her husband Kevin still live in the town where my wife was raised. It's a nice little town in East Texas, which is very different from the rest of Texas. East Texas is lush and humid and green, 'cause they've got vegetation and pollen and stuff there. It's damn near Louisiana and that's a little scary in itself.

---

[1] Oh hey, one thing real quick before I get into this too far. You know those serial killers out there: the guys that try to kill everyone? I don't know how many of you read my stuff, but just in case listen to this idea and tell me what you think.

Now I am in NO WAY asking you to do this, understand? I'm not sayin', "Go out there and do this," but you know if you're going do it anyway, you know? Hey, why not try killing people that nobody likes anyway, or people that ruin it for the rest of us? You know, like maybe —oh let's see— lawyers. Dude, just think about it for a minute. Why not kill lawyers? Pretty good idea, huh? If you're bound and determined you're going to kill somebody and I can't stop you, why not do us all a favor. And you guys that do it for sexual reasons, there sure are a lot of pretty women lawyers out there these days, you know. Aren't they really just kind of asking for it? Anyway, it's just a suggestion. Thank you. If you're an attorney, I hope I didn't offend you. And I hope you don't sue me, but you guys are just scum. There was more decency in Osama bin Laden's little penis than in your entire family tree. I can't believe Hitler didn't start with you guys first. Thank you, and now back to our story.

They've got this really nice lake house out in the woods, and sometimes my wife and I like to go there. They've got speedboats, pedal boats, jet skis, and all kinds of stuff that I don't know a lot about. Usually, I just sit on the dock, reading and waving to them as they float by.

One particular time we took The Good Dog Comet with us. Though we got him used, Comet has been around a long time now, and we let him sleep inside these days. His full name is Comet "The Wonder Dog" Pullen, though a few years back he was a bit rebellious and changed it to "The Dog Formerly Known as Comet." He replaced his name with a Milkbone symbol. Now he's just Down Home Bob, Defender of the Porch, Lord-o-the-Nap, Connoisseur of Cookies.

He's really a good dog, and as you probably already know, the winner of the 1996 coveted Dole Fruit Bar Challenge. Back in the old days, on Saturday mornings at seven thirty, the doorbell would ring and every little girl in the neighborhood would ask my wife if Comet or I could come out and play.

So, I took my good and faithful friend to the lake where he could run around and pee on everything, get petted a lot, walk in the water, and get as dirty as he wanted.[2]

Paula and Kevin have two girls, Katy and Dawn. I've been around since they were little girls. They're both well-mannered, smart, pretty, young women and I don't have a bad word to say about them; nobody could. They're both outgoing and popular in school. They both have busy

---

[2]You do know I write some of this stuff while I'm sitting in quiet little watering holes right? I just take my laptop and usually sit at the end of the bar away from everybody. I find it relaxing. I enjoy watching and listening to the people around the bar. So while I was writing, this old man walked up and looked over my shoulder. I turned around to greet him.

"Whatcha' doin', writin' a book?" he asked smiling.

"Whatchoo doin'? Messin' with a psychopath?" I was about to say, but I'd had a drink or two, so I smiled back at him. "Yeah," I said, "just messin' around."

social lives. They're just good kids and they were always good.

I have two children also, a son and a daughter. Both my children are from a previous marriage. Their mother and I divorced when they were very young. I don't think they ever remember a time in their lives when I didn't have a home away from theirs.

I had visitation with my children every other weekend, every other Christmas and Thanksgiving, and six weeks every summer. It's the same deal most non-custodial parents have. It sucked, but we survived.

It really bothered me in a lot of ways when my ex moved to a small town fifty miles from me to raise the kids in the country. I saw them a lot less, and they never dropped by, but my ex and I both thought it was better for the kids to be raised in a small town. I still do.

My second (and most current) wife and I don't have any children of our own for a number of reasons, and now it's too late 'cause we're, you know, old and barren and stuff. She's never had any children of her own, and mine were six and seven when she and I met. My kids and my new wife

---

"Wow, a writer, that's really something."

I nodded my head and took a drink. "Ya know, just because I'm writin' doesn't mean that it's any good."

"Well, I think it's really something anyway," he acknowledged.

He was a very short little man in his mid-sixties and pleasant enough. I think he would have made an excellent victim in a homicide. We introduced ourselves and he told me he was an insurance actuary.

"What the hell is that?" I responded.

He giggled a bit. "I'm the guy that computes your insurance premiums based on statistics, current trends, and other data."

"Wow, now *that's* interesting, or at least it would be if you actually used the information to assess rates, but don't you *really* use the numbers to justify an increase either way?"

He giggled again. "Bingo!" He was really quite proud of himself. "If you've never had a wreck, the odds are you're going to, so your rates go up. If you've had a lot of accidents," he continued, "the odds are you'll continue to be a high risk, so your rates go up." He smiled. "Pretty cool ,huh?"

never really formed a family bond, ya know? I mean they were nice to each other, and liked each other, but my current wife never thought of them as hers: they were always mine. And that's okay, because most likely — they are.

I don't know for sure, but I don't think it bothered my children *that* much, ya know? I mean, after all, they did have a mother and a father that loved them even though we weren't together. Besides, my ex married a young kid who turned out to be a very good influence on them. He really did a great job of raising them in my absence, and I take my hat off to the guy. He has officially become my step-husband and we both recently had the great honor of escorting my daughter down the aisle. I think *I* would have felt bad had he not been shown the respect he deserved.

I know there are people that don't, but I like to think most people want their children to be happy. Most parents try to give their children everything, every advantage they can, and I can dig that too, ya know? Sometimes it works,

---

"Yeah, what a scam," I noted. "I hope your firm is audited by Arthur Anderson, you slimy little bastard."

"Yeah!" he laughed. "I don't even know why I bother to go into work every day."

"Your children must be very proud of you," I said smiling. I mean after all, it wasn't this little piece of shit that fucked up everything. Not by himself, he wasn't that sharp. He's really just a symptom of a disease, and you and I are carriers.

Looking at the CNN reporter on the screen, he motioned with his glass towards the television at the end of the bar. "We should have government agents on each airliner with bombs," he said. They were talking about airport security.

"Bombs on airplanes? That's crazy," I threw back at him.

He giggled and leaned into me, smelling of scotch.

"Do you know the odds of a civilian airliner having *two* bombs on board at any given time?" he asked. "It's astronomical." Then he turned and shuffled back to the dumb-ass side of the bar where he belonged. Hey, I admit that I'm screwed up too, but at least I don't do it for a living — yet.

and other times you get Kennedys. No one ever knows how much is *too much*, and does it really relate to the type of person we'll grow up to be, anyway? Are these traits something more than our social upbringing? Could it be chromosomes, or peer influence, or pure chance? Who knows why we turn out the way we do? Jeffrey Dahmer's dad seems like a nice well-adjusted guy to me. What went wrong? Some people (myself included) have said, "Spare the rod and spoil the child," but there are folks that *do* spare the rod and their kids are just fine. I don't get it. And what am I supposed to do with this spare rod?

My wife and I have talked about her sister's choices over the years regarding the upbringing of her girls. Sometimes, we thought the girls were getting too much too easy, and they'd end up being little shits. Over the years, I've watched them grow up. I can't see any signs of them not being concerned, hard-working, caring, polite, young ladies. So much for my philosophy.

I guess my point is this: *these* girls were raised with all the things they could have ever wanted. They had a mother, a father, and grandparents right there with them every day of their lives. Their parents and extended family were at every piano recital, every soccer game, and every trip to the zoo.

My kids, on the other hand, had less: less money, less clothing, less fathering, less supervision, less family, less of a home. Now I'm not talking about a lot less, but clearly when compared, less.

My daughter called me that night out at the lake. It was late on Saturday night and the house was full of people. Katy had four friends staying overnight and there was so much commotion going on that I went outside to talk.

My daughter was crying because she had an argument with her roommate and she was upset. I was 120 miles away, it was eleven at night and I didn't know what I could do about it anyway. At the time the only thing I could do was listen.

So I listened to this little girl of mine who had grown up. I had noticed, over the years, that it has sometimes been difficult for my daughter to make and maintain relationships with people. There occasionally comes a time in every situation with her where things just go south. Maybe that's my influence on her, or maybe it's just her. I turned to look in the large plate-glass windows that run the length of their lake house as I listened. I could see Katy and all her friends laughing and talking. I felt a knot in my stomach.

I wished *my* daughter were as happy. I wished my daughter were at *our* lake house with all her friends laughing. I wished that I could wave a wand and make it better for her. I wished I could fix it for her. I wished I could have helped build a child who never had to be sad, was always happy, and maybe I could have — if only I'd been there. Or I'd been a better father. I realize, of course, that logically not *everything* bad in life is *entirely* my fault. I know that I tried my best at the time for what my best is worth. But I think good parents always feel pain when their children are in need. We wonder, "Could I have done more? Was I only thinking of myself when they were young?"

I'm gonna tell you something that I've never told anyone before: Once when my children were young, I took them to New Mexico to see the freaks. On the way there from Dallas we spent the night in the Texas Panhandle town of Amarillo. Now, just in case you don't know, Amarillo is just a big ol' skinny void in the Cosmos. It's like an anti-black hole because everything has to get out. It really doesn't deserve to have a name. If something is rotten in Denmark, then imagine how this place smells.

But, just a few miles outside of Amarillo, there is another hole called Palo Duro Canyon, and it's really kind of cool. Not awesome, but cool.

We drove through the canyon on our way out of Amarillo and looked at the stuff. It was okay, I guess, but the kids didn't get it. "Yeah, yeah," I'm sure they thought, "dirt, rocks, cactus, we get it."

Now, down in the bottom of this canyon, there's this little train. For some reason unbeknownst to me, the thing was called "The Monkey Train." They had brightly painted plywood cut-outs of monkeys all over the little depot/ticket booth. There were monkeys swinging through the jungle vines, and monkeys eating bananas with big, broad, toothy smiles. When my little girl saw this thing, she just lost it.

"A Monkey Train!" she shouted from the backseat of the rental car. I pulled into the small parking lot to try and figure out the allure of this cheap sideshow for my little girl. We watched the train pull out of the little station. It was a tiny little scale train like you would see at a zoo or theme park. My daughter loved it.

"Daddy, can we ride it?" she begged.

I didn't say anything. At first, I just sat there.

I couldn't see any correlation between a desert canyon and this monkey theme, but they seemed to be sellin' it.

I thought to myself, there were no monkeys in there. That was just the name because somebody got their hands on some cheap wooden cutouts with monkeys all over 'em. And they wanted ME to pay for it. It could have just as easily have been the "Taco Train!" or the "Today Only: 2 For a Dollar Train!"

It was hot. It was dusty. It was expensive. The sign said it was an eighteen minute round trip. I looked at my daughter in the backseat and then at the train chugging off in the distance. I tried to explain to her that there were probably no real monkeys on the trip, that it was just a name. Plus, it would be a LONG TIME before the train came back.

The real truth is this: I was scared to ride that stupid Monkey Train. Yeah, I said scared.

55

See, I've got this psychological/biological defect that makes me see perfectly normal or rational things as *irrational*. I have fears that are completely unfounded in merit. I don't like crowds, and being in the middle of one upsets me sometimes to the point of panic. I always need an exit in any room that I'm in, or else I feel trapped and become frantic. I, therefore, have a problem with most forms of mass transit, movie theaters, family reunions, restaurants, or stores — you name it. Sometimes I'm just afraid of the responses it triggers in me. Sometimes it's utterly overwhelming terror. Some days, you don't want to leave the security of your home. Yeah, I know it's stupid, that's why they call it irrational.

It was really bad back when my kids were little, and nobody really knew what was going on inside me. But the truth was, I was afraid and I didn't know how to explain it to my innocent daughter.

This tiny girl would sit on the couch with me and inspect my rough, wounded hands when she was but a toddler. My hands, then as they are now, are the hands of any uneducated, common working man: dry, scarred, and stained with years of ignorance.

She would look at each cut and abrasion (and there have always been many), then she would make a face full of sadness and sympathy. She would do the same for every tear and blemish she discovered. What a kid.

I like to think those cuts were for her sake, but they probably weren't.

I should have, right then like Pecos Bill, ripped up that dadburn train track like an ornery ol' rattlesnake and snapped it like my trusty bullwhip, and slung them monkeys back to the jungle where the varmints belong. Or, I wish to God now, that I'd just *ridden* that stupid train.

By the way, I'm much better nowadays. For the most part, I can do almost anything that any other normal four-year-old can do with little or no outwardly visible signs of distress. It's still in there, though, and I have to fight it every second of every day. If I hadn't told you, you wouldn't have known anything was wrong, unless I tried to kill you.

I know to all of you non-parents, some of this might sound like a crock, but it's true. This regret, this guilt, can eat some people alive from the inside. It's a cancer that grows until it controls your very existence, and even alters the *way* you think. It's just some of the price you pay for the decisions you make; it's the cost of admission.

In the Academy Award winning movie *The Mission*, Robert De Niro plays an eighteenth century Spanish slave trader in the jungles of South America. He and his brother quarreled over a candy bar or something, and Bob slew his brother. He immediately repented, and felt the need to dedicate his life to the service of the church. He loaded up all of his armor, cutlery, and other heavy tools of his former trade, and then the poor bastard dragged them through the mountainous rain forests of South America. Up slippery, steep jungle trails and across raging, treacherous rivers he trudged. He crawled while pulling, fighting, and dragging his burdens of remorse: the sharp and weighty instruments of his violent past. To him, these were the real-life symbols of his earthly sins. Sometimes I feel like that poor, tortured man, dragging the weight of every mistake or inappropriate action I've ever made into my future. Sometimes, things feel smooth and fine. I feel free. But I turn like an idiot, and suddenly they reappear. I think it's in my nature to always turn around when things are going okay. I might have accidentally used a very important chromosome as bait on a drunken fishing trip back in the '70s.

Now I don't want to bring you down, so I want you to know that everything is okay with my daughter. It was no big deal, and it's long over. She's great. She's a happily married brain surgeon, or a prison warden, or something like that, and she loves it. She's happy and I'm happy. I'm very proud of her and I still love her in some ways.[3]

Anyway, the next day at the lake was beautiful and mild. I had coffee in the morning and laughed just like a normal person. I drove my first jet ski and it was pretty cool. I took my beloved old dog out in the cove on the pedal boat. He wanted to get a duck that was swimming around out there and I told him I'd assist him in any way I could. Our original plan was to catch it, kill it, and then eat it, but I couldn't pedal fast enough to catch up with the duck. So, thinking quickly, I explained to him that duck is sometimes a little greasy, especially if it's eaten raw. In the end, we decided to let it keep swimming without fear, right in front of us and just out of our reach.

Ya know, I'd like to think that old dog will always remember the day I took him out on that boat, how close we got to that smart-ass duck, and how fun it was for him to swim in the cool water. I think it was great and I was happy for him. But, ya know, any way you look at it, he's just a dog.

There was this Greek historian named Polybius who described the way ancient societies swore pledges of treaties or made oaths to one another. He wrote this:

> The man who is swearing to the treaty takes in his hand a stone, and when he has taken the oath in the name of his country, he says: "If I abide by this oath, may all good be my lot; but if I do otherwise in thought or act, let all other men dwell safe in their own countries enjoying their own laws and in possession of their own property — and may I alone be cast out even as this stone is now." Then having spoken these words, he throws the stone from his hand.

I've always thought that was a cool oath and for some

---

[3]I'm kidding.

reason it hits home. I don't know, maybe it's the "time for casting away stones" analogy that I like, but anyway, here's my deal: if you guys buy my stuff and I get paid for this story, I swear I'll take the oath above, and I'll *really* mean it this time. I don't mean like Stephen King kind of money either. You know, just a few mil here and there is plenty. I promise I will take a reasonable percentage of the proceeds and I will personally go buy a cool boat and a trailer. AND I will also buy a reliable new vehicle (with A/C and a six-disk CD changer) to pull the boat around. But (and here's the great part) I promise I'LL never touch it. I'll have it parked under a shelter, keep it gassed up and clean and ready to go twenty-four hours a day, seven days a week, fifty-two weeks a year — for you. It'll all be free. We'll even have a person who answers the phone and reserves the boat. She'll be good looking, too. I think it'd be cool if we could book it every day of the year. I want you to take your kids, your wives, your boyfriends or both, (and your dogs) out for a day or two.

It'll be our insurance, our excuse eliminator. Just think of it, you'll never again be able to say to your kids, "We can't."

Maybe we can also have a fund to pay for those guys that say, "Daddy can't, he has to work." I mean come on, cut the crap, no bullshit, I don't care if you're shy, or what *your* personal problems might be, just get your lazy, worthless, self-centered ass out there and do it. You'll thank me later. I don't even care if you're afraid. You know, friend, even the pyramids of Egypt will someday just be fodder for a footpath. All we really have that is lasting is our sheer existence. What we do with this existence might possibly be remembered. Occasionally, we do get second chances. Sometimes, even as adults, we're allowed a few do-overs.

If you're not gonna live some semblance of an existence, then go ahead and just do us all a big favor and check out early. You're probably right, you're probably not needed anyway. It's okay, you can leave, you may be excused. You won't be missed.

I think I can hear the Monkey Train coming back down the line. Come on man, don't be a spectator.

Ride, swim, live.

COLORADO STORY #105

We Are Sorry

Colorado Story #105 is
temporarily closed for
renovations.
Please feel free to visit one
of our other fine Colorado
stories.

Colorado Story #106

Y a know, I think I should really write this story down before I fall over dead in some bar with drool dripping from my mouth. The other patrons will probably watch and wonder if I'm really going to be needing that beer I just ordered, or maybe some stupid son of a bitch will shoot my worthless ass just for being so good looking. Anyway — wait a second — oh man, for a minute I thought that guy over there had a gun, but it was just a knife. [1]

Anyway, the year was 1973 and I was living in Austin, Texas. Now, I wasn't really "living" in the sense that a decent person like you would recognize. All I was really doing was spending my student loan on drinking, writing some really lame songs, and getting laid. It was nice while it lasted though, and I've recently applied for a new loan.

I was walking down Nueces Street one night on my way to my girlfriend's[2] apartment, when I noticed a new club had sprung up in what had previously been an abandoned nineteenth century house just the day before.

I went up the creaking old steps and entered the gutted dwelling to find a nice, little wooden bar and perhaps twenty tables with an assortment of cheap, used chairs. It looked like my kind of place, it had a roof and everything.

---

[1] Oh, and Buford, or Cletus, or whatever your white trash hillbilly name is, there is absolutely nothing about Arkansas in this story. So you can just put this down right now and walk away. There are no pictures for you to look at either, so leave me alone and quit bothering the other people — I've told you before I don't have any stories about Arkansas. I don't know much about the place. I don't want to know more about the place, AND I WILL NEVER write a story about the place. Okay?

[2] By the way, this particular girlfriend is now very famous and you've seen her on TV. Send $19.95 (+ $5 S&H) for your own set of nude photos.

After some serious deliberation I decided to have a beer or two, but I knew I needed to clear out early because I had a plane to catch for Dallas early the next morning.

On a large chalkboard with a clip-light, right below their menu of veggie burgers, I noticed they had a schedule of upcoming local performers. Thursday was *Johnny Vanderver and the Ewing Street Times (featuring Shake Russell)*. It was Thursday. Cool.

I had seen this band quite a few times back in Dallas and at a dozen clubs in Austin. I always enjoyed listening to them. The first time I caught them it was *Johnny Vandiver and The Ewing Street Times*, but the band later hired a round-faced kid with braces and wiry hair that stuck out in all directions. It made him look like he had the absolute biggest head of any human ever born, or that ever will be. His head looked like a giant M&M with a little hair on it. His name was Shake Russell, and he wrote and sang the most beautiful ballads I had ever heard. It didn't take long for Shake to start amassing his own following of fans.

On or about my tenth beer, the band arrived and set up. I recognized a lot of the people in the audience, as we all loved folk music, and I suspected strongly that we were all drunks.

There was one guy in particular whom I had seen everywhere that I had seen this band. I had met him a few times, his name was Francisco. When he saw me, he took a seat at my table and we talked about the music scene. I didn't know what his deal was, whether he was a musician himself, a wannabe, or just a real fan of that kind of music, 'cause he was EVERYWHERE I went, I mean EVERYWHERE.

To make a short story shorter, we talked, we drank, we listened, blah, blah, blah, 'nuff said. So when the money was gone, and I didn't want to wait for ATMs to be invented, I bid a fond adieu to Francisco, tipped my hat to the band, and split. I'm sure I made my way home or I wouldn't be here to tell you this. I must have gotten up the next day, 'cause I'm sure I did, otherwise — oh, never mind.

The next morning, I might have overslept, or some worthless friend who I can't even remember didn't pick me up — or some other crap like that happened. Bottom line, I missed my flight to Dallas. I had to get to Colorado to visit some musician friends that were playing there for a few days. Now, this was a royal pain, because I needed to catch another flight at Love Field that afternoon, which would somehow get me to Denver, and then to some small town somewhere in the rocks called Breckenridge. It was supposed to be "quaint," and "scenic," and "cold." I didn't really care 'cause it wasn't really my money. Slinging my duffle bag over my shoulder, I grabbed my guitar and banjo, and hit Nineteenth Street.

I wasn't on the street but a few seconds before some nice housewife-type lady picked me up, and took me to the interstate (I'd really like to say that she and I hit it off and we enjoyed the beauty and spirit of the moment and spent a blissful time of togetherness in celebration — our love was a mutual and caring expression of our deep, inner feelings — mutual respect and nurturing — with quick arrow-like thrusts — anyway, we didn't). She was nice and she just gave me a ride to the highway, okay? So get off my ass.[3]

I was just on the edge of Austin's polite society when an old, small, blue Ford pulled over in the breakdown lane and waited for me. I could see through the rear window that its driver was a single female. I approached the passenger side and smiled into the open window.

---

[3]Ya know, about the Arkansas thing earlier, the more I think about it, I really don't know if I've ever even been there for sure. Okay, once I might have driven across there to get to a real place like Memphis or something, but I'm sure I would have never actually touched it or anything like that. I also think I vaguely remember navigating a large vessel of some sort from the Gulf of Mexico upstream and waving at a bunch of dumb-asses, but I don't think that legally constitutes "contact."

A twenty-something black girl gave me a sultry grin and said, "Hop on in, honey." I threw my stuff on top of her stuff in the backseat, and wormed my way into the cramped cab.

Her name was Jennifer and she was heading Waco-ward, same as me. She wore an extremely short, loose-fitting summer dress with buttons all the way down the front. It might have been a bit "out of season" considering it was December, but I didn't know it. The weather was pleasant.

She spoke loudly as we cruised, continuously popping piece after piece of hard candy into her mouth from a bag nestled between her legs. She pointed to the open bag at one point and asked, "You want some?"

I smiled, "No, thanks."

Ya know, I was pretty young back then and the world had just started to grow up. There was a lot of new stuff going on out there, but this was a new one to me; a little confusing, but there was something in her tone that didn't seem right.

I could tell her hair wasn't real, but that was not uncommon at the time for black females. Maybe the difference was that her wig touched the cloth interior of the roof of the cab and I could see her bare legs were longer and more muscular than mine. Also, I felt kinda strange when she would scan me up and down slowly, then smile while speaking in a flirtatious manner. I think what first started me wondering was her deep, low voice. I swear, if I closed my eyes, this woman sounded just like a man. Isn't that weird?

You've got to remember that this was the early '70s and there had never been a transsexual, transvestite, drag queen, female impersonator, or anything else remotely associated with this kind of business in the history of all mankind. Hell, the first documented case of homosexuality was not even reported until what — the early '80s? So this was really big. This was the forefront of Western societal sexual trends, and once again I was there first. It did feel a little creepy in such tight quarters with someone who could, and would, smother me with affection. But I was a bold adventurer, an explorer, a jet-setting guy on the go. I was hip.

"So," she asked with a grin, "how far do you wanna go, sugar?"

I glanced out the window and pointed to the green sign that slid by. "Oh, there's my exit now."

I walked for an exit or two before a nondescript rental car commanded by an extremely large, white man picked me up. He was probably six foot two, 240 pounds, crew-cut, fortyish, wearing a white, pullover knit-shirt with a collar. He was a sergeant in the Army and heading back to his base in Oklahoma. I'd be willing to bet he was probably a male. I thought he was pretty cool to pick up a nineteen-year-old long-haired hippie.

We also stopped and picked up a young soldier along the way. I sat and listened to them talk in Greek about military stuff all the way to Dallas.

The sergeant and I dropped off the soldier on the outskirts of Dallas and then we stopped at my parent's house to see if anyone there could shuttle me to the airport for my flight to Denver, but no one was home. The sergeant came in and we ate a sandwich at my mom's house. When he was finished, he split and was last seen heading north on I-35. There are those that say they still see him to this day driving up and down that old highway.

I decided to call my ex-girlfriend Penny to see if she could take off from work and give me a lift to the airport. She told me she'd be glad to take off and give me a ride, as long as my destination was Hell.

It was only about twelve miles to Love Field, Dallas's main airport at the time, so I decided to call a taxi. For a brief moment, I considered leaving my guitar, or at least my banjo, at my parents' house, 'cause man, I was carrying a lot of stuff around, but I figured from here on out I'd have porters and servants and stuff carry my junk for me. So when he arrived to collect me, I threw them in the cab.

The guy got me there just in time for my two o'clock flight. I ran through the airport with all my shit, and still managed to look extremely cool. Once onboard, I slid into a nice comfy seat, and knew the worst was finally behind me.

On the plane I met this guy who was from Colorado Springs (in Colorado). I couldn't get him to shut up. He told me about his lame job. He told me about his stupid wife and his dumb kids; shit like that. Oh yeah, and hummingbirds. This guy loved hummingbirds. Everything he said for about twenty minutes was about hummingbirds. I really don't remember much else about what he said, I mean, it wasn't as if we were talking about anything important, like me or something.[4]

Anyway, I did the ol' phone number exchange with him and promised I'd keep in touch (as if my phone would still be working when I got back home).

We had to stop in Colorado Springs to let Mr. Numbnuts off (like he couldn't have walked the mile and a half from Denver). I just hope he's happy there in his beautiful Colorado Springs: THE CHILD MOLESTATION CAPITAL OF THE WORLD.[5] There, with his little retarded family, blissfully unaware of the pain he'd caused others. Hopefully his rotting corpse is being picked clean in some Middle Eastern country by the elusive, yet deadly *Hummingbore Saurus* (Humming Lizard).

---

[4]Just a little side note here: I didn't want to hurt Mr. I'm-in-Sales-and-I-Don't-Know-How-to-Shut-Up's feelings, but he didn't know shit about hummingbirds. It just so happens that I am one of the world's foremost experts on the subject, but I didn't want to, you know — what's the word? — "encourage" him. For example: did you know it's a fact that hummingbirds don't have any legs? It's weird, but true. They're like snakes and stuff: they have to crawl around on their stomachs, like a walrus or something. Have you ever seen one walkin' around? Did you know that in Greenland, hummingbirds look EXACTLY like regular birds? One last bit of hummingbird trivia I find extremely interesting is the fact that they spend their entire lives without ever touching the earth. If a hummingbird ever touches the ground, you have to burn them. For more information concerning hummingbirds or any other kind of reptiles, just log onto my website.

[5]Note to Editor: be sure and check this before publication.

We landed ten minutes later in Denver in the middle of a blizzard. Everybody was swarming around the counters and camping out in their sleeping bags on the floor. All the flights in and out were cancelled, and everybody was freaking out. I couldn't believe they had come to Colorado in December and had not expected to see some snow. Help me, it's a blizzard, ooh, I'm so scared! What a bunch of dumb-asses. I am *so* glad I'm me.

I laughed and shook my head as I stepped up to the little kiosk with a cute woman behind the counter. "I need a car." I smirked as I leaned my pile of shit against the counter.

She looked up at me and swept her hair from her face. "What?" she asked.

I could tell she was digging me and trying to hide her obvious fascination by acting on edge and short of temper. I placed my forearms on the counter and did my eye contact thing. "I'd like to get a nice car, please. What do you think, maybe a convertible? — red preferably."

She continued staring at me with her mouth slightly open. She brushed her hair back again. "You do understand it's snowing outside, don't you?" she asked.

"Oh, yeah," I said, using my second best smile, "never mind about the convertible." I looked around to see if any of the other car rental agencies had a more attractive counter girl, or at least one more willing to give in to her true feelings regarding her attraction to me. Dude, she was getting desperately close to being on the verge of losing her big chance, if you know what I mean.

She just kept staring at me. "What are you some kind of dumb-ass or something?" she eventually said with genuine interest. Finally! See I told you she was interested, because she glanced down at her clipboard for a second and looked back up. "Do you see all these people here, sir?"

I looked around at all the folks in the terminal, nodding my head 'cause I did see all the people there. "Yeah, this is hip, everybody all together and groovin'. Cool."

"We're in the middle of a blizzard, you idiot," she said.

"Right on. I can dig it, mama," I said all cool and everything, but I was getting a little tired of her trip. "I'm hip. I can dig your scene. You guys have a great time, okay. Now can I have my car or what?"

I think I heard her say something like, "What are you, like sixteen or something? Get outta here." So I left that lesbian and her lonely pathetic life in my past. You have to admit though, at least I tried. I gave her a chance and she blew it.

I kind of pushed my stuff on the slick marble floor towards the exit doors and piled it all up in the covered pick-up/drop-off area, and sat down to think about what to do next. It was after five o'clock and getting dark. I looked for a cab, but some guy told me there were no taxis out because they were afraid of the weather. What a bunch of pussies.

There were busses idling all over the place. Some of them were shuttle busses with the names of resorts posted on their sides and the lighted plates up on top. But I didn't know any of the places they advertised, and I hate to ask people how to do stuff, and I really didn't know how busses worked, ya know?

I'd never really looked at a map of Colorado before and I didn't know exactly where Denver was or its relationship to Breckenridge. I just figured I'd find it, ya know? I sat there for about an hour and thought about it. I don't think anybody knew I didn't know what I was doing, which was my intent. Finally, a bus pulled in with the words "Grand Junction" on it. Now that was more like it. That's exactly what I needed, a *grand junction*. A "junction," if you don't know, is a place where they have taxis and rental cars and ice cream and stuff. It's close to everything; that's why they call it a junction and *this* one must really be a good one, for it was a GRAND JUNCTION.

I walked up to the bus with some of my stuff. The driver

was loading bags and boxes into a cargo bay underneath the bus. I thought about letting him have some of my things to make it easier on me, but I didn't want my guitar or banjo exposed to the slush and snow, so I carried them onboard and stuck them in a seat at the back of the bus. When I came back out to get the rest of my things, he was still bent over shoving and arranging stuff in the cargo hold, so I guess maybe he didn't see me get on the first time.

I finally got the last of my crap on board and went to the back where I sat in the dark. It was nice, cozy, and warm. While waiting for the conductor to come and get my money I looked around for the stewardess so I could get a buzz going, but I couldn't see her either. So I sat there and waited quietly for them to serve dinner, without a drink or nothing. I was gonna get up at one point and jump the driver's shit 'cause I'd been sitting there for like five minutes or so. I really wanted to get going soon, but I figured I'd just go along with the program and try to be cooperative. It was the least I could do since they were all so upset about the weather. I guess we've all got to sacrifice sometimes and I was like, you know, willing to do my part for the greater good and stuff.

A family from Texas got on board and sat down in my area and we started to shoot the shit. They were from Houston, a small town down on the coast of Texas known for absolutely nothing. I knew the place well as I had stopped there once to throw up on my way to Galveston.

They had a couple of kids along with them that were in their early teens and they had come to Colorado to go snow skiing. When I heard that, I knew through sheer deductive reasoning (of which I am a master) that they were going to be in or near the mountains. As I was hopefully heading that way, I decided I'd discreetly follow them.

I also noticed, in the dim light of the bus, that one of the kids didn't have an ear. Well, I mean he *had* an ear — but he also *didn't* have an ear. He only had one AND he was missing one, too (also). I can't remember which was missing and which was there, but I guess that's not all that important to anyone but him. His brother (the one without the foot) was seated across the aisle from him, and he had shot off his brother's ear in a hunting accident.

"So, other than shooting your brother," I inquired, "did you have any luck?"

"Yeah," their father stated proudly, "Todd got a buck."

The other boy said, "Huh?"

The man and lady were real party types and soon they busted out a nice big bottle of Jack Daniels. The guy's wife even had a stack of plastic cups and a small ice chest full of ice and, as fate would have it, I had conveniently brought a mouth (oh, that reminds me to tell you about the third kid), so we were in business.

As we crept along the interstate, I asked them quietly if they knew which part of the mountain range Breckenridge was in. They told me I needed to get off the bus *before* Grand Junction, at a place called Frisco. They weren't even going all the way to the junction either, but to some town called Vail. I didn't get it. Why'd they even bother putting "Grand Junction" on the sign if that's not where we were going?

The more I drank, the more I got pissed off that the driver had screwed up so badly. I was determined to let him know that *I* knew he had messed everything up (word of advice here, don't ever think about trying to pull the wool over my eyes, you'll only be wasting your time). I thought to myself, wouldn't it be cool under the circumstances to tear into him all mad and stuff. So I had another drink and bid my time. I figured I'd probably look a lot sharper if I only berated him verbally, without you know, getting physical with him.

I looked out the window and saw a sign in the gloom and falling snow that said "Georgetown 6 miles, Frisco 34 miles." I knew this guy'd never figure out his problem if I didn't set him straight. So I took a big drink and made my way up the aisle to the front of the bus. I stood next to him, sipped my drink, and watched this idiot try to keep the bus on the road. I shook my head. Man, he was like, incompetent or something, ya know?

"Snowin' pretty bad out there, isn't it?" I commented.

He jumped with a start and turned his glance up to me quickly and then back to the snow covered road. Man, you could hardly even see out those big 'ol windows in the front of the bus.

"Sir," he said sweating, all nervous and everything, "we're in a blizzard. Please take your seat immediately."

I smiled. He *knew.* He knew I was onto him. I put my left hand on the back of his seat and leaned over into his ear. "You know," I said matter-of-factly, "you fucked up pretty bad back there in Denver." I smiled. "I'm not going to the junction, I'm going to Frisco."

He glanced from side to side out the windows and then looked me up and down real quick. "What's your problem, man?"

I smiled. "Listen pal, just let me off at Frisco and we'll forget about you tryin' to take me to a junction when I didn't even need to go there. Okay?"

He looked me in the eye. "Who are you?"

"Oh, you'll find out," I cried as I headed back to my seat.

"Sir!"

I turned and walked back. "Yeah, what is it?" I had already decided I wasn't going to accept any excuses or apologies.

"You got a ticket to be on this bus?" he asked, looking me in the face.

I laughed. "Duh, no I don't! *That's* another thing you forgot to do." I smiled and shook my head, then I gave him a mock sympathy pat on the back. "I'm sure glad I'm not in your shoes, pal. This isn't going to look good on your record."

I went to the rear of the bus and started gathering all my stuff up in a pile. I admit I felt a little sorry for the guy, but dammit, he had to learn. Actually, in a way, I probably did him a big favor in the long run.

A couple of minutes later we pulled off the highway at Georgetown, which by the way, was not even a scheduled stop. The Georgetown Police, Grand County Sheriff, and a Clear Creek County Sheriff's deputy were waiting. They all just stood there in the snow smiling, and then helped me get all my stuff off the bus.

Now I know you're going to find this hard to believe, but in Colorado (The forty-ninth poorest state in the union) you're supposed to buy your bus ticket at a "ticket counter." Then you're supposed to give the ticket to the driver as you board. You're supposed to tell the "ticket agent" where you want to go and she gives you a "ticket" to give to the driver. The driver also receives from the "ticket agent" a passenger and destination list.

Is that not the stupidest system you've ever heard of? What about all those old movies where the conductor walks through the train shouting, "Tickets! Get your ticket here!" Or something like that. A train is like a bus, right? They both got engines. They both got tracks. They're really the same thing, if you think about it. Am I right or what? They're exactly the same thing. Ask any four-year-old in Texas, they'll tell you they're the same thing. Man, don't they ever watch old movies in Colorado? What are you guys, a bunch of illiterates?

Because of the blizzard, the cops took me into a little diner that was right there at the exit off the interstate. I was technically between two different counties, they said, and once the bus exited the interstate I was in the incorporated township of Georgetown, Colorado. I didn't really understand all that legal crap, so I just stood there. I tried to explain about the train and how conductors are supposed to act, but they just looked at each other like a bunch of retards. One of them got some sort of a judge on the phone at the cashier's counter. I heard the cop ask him what they should do. The judge wanted to talk to me, so I got on the phone.

He asked me what was wrong with me and I shrugged

my shoulders. He said, "Are you stupid or something? Don't you understand there's a blizzard going on?"

I fired back with both guns and gave him a savagely berating, "Duh," and rolled my eyes to accentuate my point. I think they all got my meaning. Then they all just kinda looked at each other. I think it went right over their heads.

"Where are you from, son?"

"Dallas."

"Oh," and he asked to speak with one of the officers again. After a minute, the officer covered the phone receiver, "You wanna plead guilty, son?"

"To what charge?"

"Just plead guilty, otherwise we'll have to arrest you and put you in jail, give you an attorney, and he's in Orlando."

"I don't know what to do. What's the charge?"

The cop turned his back to the little group and talked to the judge some more on the phone. Finally, he turned back to me. "Speeding, the bus was going too fast."

"We couldn't have been doing even forty miles an hour!" I insisted.

He shook his head. "No, there's a blizzard going on, that's too fast. So you're guilty." He looked at his watch.

"Well, I guess I *was* speeding under the circumstance," I confessed. "Okay, I'm guilty."

The cop said "guilty" into the receiver, hung up the phone, and then turned to face me. "A $100 fine and $20 court cost," he said and rapped his flashlight on the cashier's counter so hard the gum display jumped.

I reached in my wallet and pulled out a hundred-dollar bill and a twenty. I handed the money towards the cop. He held his hands up to ward off the money. "Whoa. I can't take that! You owe — ah — $33.33 to the town of Georgetown, $33.33 to the County of Clear Lake, and $33.33 to Grand County. I can't touch *their* money." He pointed to the other officers.

"So, how much do I owe you?"

"$33.33," he said.

I looked back in my wallet. I had another hundred-dollar note, several twenties, and a few smaller bills. I handed him two twenties.

He took them and placed it in his wallet. He said, "Goodnight," and headed towards the door.

"Excuse me," I said, "my change? You forgot my change."

He stopped and looked at me and said, "I'm sorry, I can't make change. You'll have to see the county clerk on Monday, if they're open."

"Any of you other guys got change?" They all just smiled and shook their heads.

I turned to the cashier and asked her if she had change for a hundred. She just laughed, "Hon, I've got less than thirty dollars in here."

I reached in my wallet for all my twenties. I had five left. I gave forty dollars to the second officer; he tipped his hat to me and left. Then I turned to the last two guys. I gave one officer two twenties and he handed one of them to his partner. These two just stood there looking at me. One said, "Court cost $20." I handed him my last twenty-dollar bill and he stuck it in the cashier's tip jar.

"Thanks for the use of the phone Clara," he said and they walked out.

I zombied out to the light in the parking lot, dragging my duffel bag in the snow. I watched the cops in their nice, warm cars. I watched them sip on their nice, warm coffee by the green light of their instrument panels. They started to pull onto the service road in single file, each one of them heading in a different direction. When the last car was pulling out it did a U-turn and ended up two inches from my frozen toes. He cranked his window down and winced back from the bitter cold. He pulled his cheeks up to cover his eyes and, for just an instant, I think he became Clint Eastwood.

"Where you trying to get to, Tex?" he shouted over his heater blower.

"Breckenridge," I said and leaned into the warmth escaping from his open window. "Colorado," I added with a 40 percent reduction in my smart-ass tone.

He rolled a toothpick around in his mouth and glanced around the parking lot. "Get your stuff."[6]

Anyway, the cop was pretty cool, I guess. The cop, or deputy, or whatever he was, was a pretty quiet guy though. He didn't say much as we rolled along the snow. It was really falling down outside and I couldn't make out where the road was exactly. The snowflakes burst from the darkness into the field of our headlights like an explosion, and then smashed against the windshield in a kind of white,

---

[6]Excuse me, but you know the more I think about it the more I realize that the *only* thing I really know for sure about Arkansas is the unusual fact that they put the butter or jelly or whatever they are eating at the time, ON THE BOTTOM of the bread. Now to me, that's weird. It's hard to observe them doing this because every time someone from one of the other states walks into a restaurant they quickly turn their bread/toast right side up.

Oh, oh, one last thing — help me settle a bet real quick, would ya? Hey, what color is a spaceship? White, if they're from Earth, right? I called my drunken dumb-ass-neighbor Karl the other day and asked him, and he replied, "They can be any color, but if they're from outer space they're usually gold."

Gold! Have you ever heard such complete bullshit in your life?

Once, I got a couple of Malibu lights out of the front flowerbed and glued them together, so they looked like a flying saucer. I painted them gold and hung them from a tree limb with clear fishing line. Then I said to the kids in the neighborhood, "Look! What's that in the air?" and pointed at the floating disk.

Hannah (who was probably one of Karl's *own* kids) said, "It's one of those things from your garden."

See. Everyone knows spaceships from Earth are WHITE, and if they're from Mars or some other place, they're SILVER. That's how the space guys know who the good guys are. (Karl, I don't know for sure, but I bet missiles from Uranus are brown).

monochromatic psychedelic show, only to be scraped like bowling pins an instant later and replaced by a new barrage. It was the ending of *2001*, dude.

After about half-an-hour or so of travel at 20 miles per hour, a few glowing lights appeared in the near distance. Slowly, what I could make of the road died into a small building, like a lodge or something, with a flattened roof piled high with layers of smooth, level snow. Through the windows, I could see the movements of people inside and the flicker of shadows bouncing on the walls. The windows of the little building were made up of hundreds of individual diamond-shaped panes, and they sparkled from the light within. The bottom portion of each of the diamonds held an equal handful of bluish-white caked frosting. The cop pulled right up to the front door and threw the car in park.

"Is this Breckenridge?" I asked him, but he just opened the door and stepped out, then he turned back and signaled for me to follow him.

He pulled open a screen door and we walked through a small hallway full of damp coats and boots. At the end of this corridor we passed through a paned glass door. In the lobby we found eight or ten young people (maybe my age, only different in some way) sitting around talking, laughing, and sipping drinks. There was a large fire roaring in a great stone fireplace on the opposite wall. There were board games on card tables and a record spinning on a small, portable record player. They looked up from their bowls of popcorn and smiled with stuffed mouths at yours truly and my escort.

"Bert!" they all acknowledged; the lot nodding and smiling in unison. The cop removed his gloves and scooped up a handful of popcorn and began tossing the kernels into his mouth. A moment later, an older lady with a white lacy apron entered the room from the common dining area. Man, I swear she looked and acted just like Aunt Bee. She walked up to the cop and hugged him. I looked around for Barney or Thelma Lou.

"You got any room left?" he asked the little lady, pointing to me with his cupped hand. "All the roads are closed from here on."

Aunt Bee looked me over and smiled, even though I could tell she was somewhat displeased with her findings. She pointed in the direction of a large sofa packed full of clean-cut, smiling faces and I'm telling you, they smiled even more. There were teeth all over the place. Maybe this was some sort of Young Demerol Convention, I told myself.

She put her arms around me and squeezed tight. "Well, we might have to put you on the couch, but that'll be just fine, won't it?" she decided.

I smiled and nodded, "Yes, ma'am," and all the young people smiled and nodded with me. Just for my own information, I nodded once for no reason and noted they all nodded in return yet again.

After a bit the cop left me, so I made a defensive fort and sat near the front door in the middle of my possessions. I was careful to keep my back away from the Children of the Damned. I figured, I could at least get out with my guitar if I had to make a break for it. All the shiny, happy, young people came up to me and asked me questions, and smiled and offered me drinks and snacks. I accepted a few of the offerings and then hunkered back into my fortress of solitude. I never found out who those people were that fateful night or why they were so damn happy, but I am still affected strangely by it and I still get chills when I see people smile. Looking back, there was a good chance that, on that night, Bert the Cop might have accidentally driven off the map of the known universe, and that all those young folks were really Mexican (or something like that).

I leaned for a while against my duffel bag and watched the snow accumulate on the windowsills and vehicles outside. There was a yellow colored light out in the small parking lot and it gave the snowfield a soft, warm, comforting glow. I had to get out of here.

An hour of guarded terror passed when suddenly I saw a light flash across the room. Its source was from the outside world. I craned my neck so I could see out the large window. Before me was a large vehicle of some sort. It looked kinda like a street cleaner and I asked one of Satan's Children what the thing was. He bent near the window and peered out a moment, smiled and said, "Oh, that's the snowplow."

"Hey," I asked him, "where are we?"

"Frisco," he answered, still watching the snowplow.

"Where's Breckenridge?" I asked. He pointed off to the right and added, "I think that's where the snowplow is heading." He then straightened up and took a sip of his drink and floated away without his feet touching the floor.

I jumped up, dashed outside into the snow and ran up to the big, loud machine. I waved at the operator inside the cab, and he came to a stop and then shut down the thundering engine. He swung open a little glass hatch.

"Yeah?" he called across the control panel.

"You going to Breckenridge with this thing?"

He nodded and gave me *that* look. "Why?"

I made up a quick lie about my mother's failing health, because I knew that if he started the engine again my plan would be foiled. Eventually, he took pity and gave in.

"Come on," he relented and then fired the monster back up.

I couldn't believe it, what a dumb-ass. I motioned for him to wait and I ran in and grabbed my things. I should have torched the place right then, but I started back to the plow as quick as I could, dragging all my stuff.

I could tell by his expression that he was not well pleased by the volume of my luggage and he shouted down to me, "Throw that crap on the outside behind the cab."

"You have the voice of a little girl," I laughed as I climbed in with my bags. He just sat there lookin' like a big ol' gorilla staring at me (The scientific term for his affliction is called "semi-apian").

"Hey," he tried again and I laughed again.

"Man, have you ever heard yourself?" I interrupted, pulling in my banjo. "Seriously man, you got a girl's voice." I shook my head and got as comfortable as I could in the tiny control cab.

"Your stuff needs to be outside," he repeated (I could tell he was trying to make his voice lower).

"Can't," I said, patting my guitar case, "it's a Martin. We'll be fine."

He must have really known his guitars 'cause he shook his head in complete surrender and said, "Oh, it's a Martin." Or *maybe* he was just really stupid. After all, he was just a snowplow operator.

Finally, we lurched forward and into the frozen, dull wilderness. The machine threw the great mounds of snow beneath us high into the air and then off to our right. It was really pretty neat, but I checked my enthusiasm, because — in case you don't savvy — that open mouth stuff doesn't sell well in Cool World.

The two-lane blacktop I was told we were on followed a winding, frozen riverbed. In the hillside on our left, he pointed out the remains of old, long abandoned mine shafts. It was a shame that the smooth, clean, and safe route was *behind* us all the way into town. Breckenridge was only about nine miles down this road, but it took us over an hour to trudge through the drifts.

I looked ahead and saw a small, gold mining town open up before us. It was like a movie set, a Deadwood kinda town. We drove down the middle of the main street in the quiet of the dark night. I felt like Paladin riding into Dodge to settle the score and bring the desperados to justice (and get laid).

Ernie, the plow guy, shut down some big motor and the snow stopped flying in our wake and we rumbled through the quiet street. The snowplow slowed and veered to the right, pulling up next to the wooden planks of the sidewalk in front of an old two-story, western-style building. I climbed down and Ernie helped me with my stuff. It was like getting off the stagecoach in Tombstone.

Behind me I could hear familiar music playing, and when I turned I could see the backs of the band members through the large saloon-style plate glass window. The sign read: The St. Bernard Inn. I had made it.

I pushed and dragged my stuff the last few feet in the door and glanced around the crowded, cozy, candle-lit room. The place was carpeted and had red-and-white-checkered vinyl table covers, and all of them were covered with beautiful cocktails and some of the vessels had steam rising from them — just like in the pictures. Some of the folks looked over and took note of me, and then quickly turned their attention back to the stage where my friends were kicking ass.

I surveyed the faces until I spotted Francisco. He looked up and nodded. Like I said, man, that guy was EVERYWHERE. I took a seat at his table and ordered the first of several beers.[7]

---

[7]You know, most of this story is bullshit. I made it up to sound more exciting than it really was. I lied to you and now I feel bad about it. The only part of this tale that was true was the bit about Francisco.

THE LITTLE BLACK GLOVE STORY

One commonplace sight in New York City is the fact that you constantly observe gloves lying on the sidewalks when it's cold outside. On a good day you will see maybe twenty-five if you look hard enough. I've noticed they're almost always black for some reason. So I bent down and scooped up one of these wayward orphans on Lexington Avenue one Friday night, and walked into a strange tavern where I placed it on the bar. The bartender looked at me and then the dark woolen item. "Hey," I wondered aloud, "did anybody in here lose a glove?"

A normal person might have thought I was an idiot, but bartenders are a special lot. If they're any good, they're very sharp and they've already heard it all. My guy, right on cue, picked it up and examined it closely with a show of great concern, then took the gag to one of his boisterous regulars.

"Al," he called pointing to me, "this gentleman found a glove, do you know whose it might be?"

Al took the glove with a grin and ran with it, so to speak. He went from party to party at the bar and a few tables near the bar, like Prince Charming, looking for the owner of the lost glove. More than a few of the patrons actually tried it on, all adding their own humorous comments. Of course, the topic made sideways action with O.J. Simpson observances. One guy asked in a loud tipsy voice, "Wasn't this the glove Michael Jackson wore on Wednesdays?"

Three or four beers later the glove made its way around the bar and back to me. There it rested before me for a while, quite content. I put it in my coat pocket as I prepared to leave and then I made my way towards the door. The bartender called out to me, "Let's give the glove a hand!" and a few people applauded politely as I exited.

I walked alone crosstown towards Times Square with the wind howling. My face was numb. I slowed, then paused and brought forth the Bic knock-off lighter my mom had given me for my twelfth birthday and fired one up. When I was sure no one was watching, I stood in the dark for a moment then tossed the black glove back to its place on the frozen pavement.

What other common lonely glove, I wondered, could have brought so much happiness to so many people? So, I left it there for the next guy. Dude, am I cool or what?[1]

---

[1]An interesting side note: I later found the original owner of the lost glove. By sheer chance, I met him in a small bar in Kansas. I found it most astonishing that he had never even been to New York — wow, is that weird or what?

Rusty and Me[1]

1

I've always suspected that it was inevitable. I knew the day would come in a moment of personal weakness, and I've dreaded this day for many years — and now it's time has come. I tried to protect you for as long as I could, but I knew there would come a time when I'd tell you about Rusty and me — and I'm sorry.

Okay, here's the scoop. It was around some time and I was in the process of completing the second leg of

---

[1] Oh by the way, if Rusty or even Mike, for that matter, ever try to write their own stories about back then, don't believe them. They'd probably lie to you and try to make it look like they were the cool ones. You should play your cards wisely and stick with a proven winner.

my scholastic tour of the entire second-rate academic institutions of the country. At the time I'm referring to, I had landed back in my hometown of Dallas. Mike, my musician friend from previous stories, and I were both booked at the same nightclub for several months — and it was great. Mike and I had been best friends since about the fourth grade and were fierce competitors. We were scheduled on an every-other-night basis. Mike would play, say, Tuesday, Thursday, Saturday, while I would perform on Monday, Wednesday, and Friday. We both had some quiet nights early in the week and we both had a weekend night, but this story is not about Mike and me, it's about Rusty and me.

The place was called Mazo's Pub and it was absolutely wild. It attracted clientele from a diverse cross section. We had intellectual biker types, music connoisseurs, barroom philosophers, and a shitload[2] of soon-to-be ex-SMU students.

Mike and I were very well matched during this era and it was an interesting study in human behavior. We were both solid acts even as young boys (as an infant I had a steady gig at The Frontier Room in the Poconos with Vic Damon and Martin and Lewis). Mike could play the guitar the first time he looked at one in early grade school. Not only was he a child virtuoso, but he hadn't bothered to learn how to play one either. I swear before Almighty God that he played as well the first time he touched it as he does today. I don't mean this as an insult, but he hasn't gotten one bit better in over forty years. He was already the best, but it really doesn't matter much to this story because it's not about him, it's really about Rusty.

I don't want to go on all day about this (because of the above reason), but it was an amazing thing to witness, nonetheless. He never learned the chords or their names, he just played them. Sometimes the fingering was wrong, but

[2]Although "shitload" is a scientific unit of measure with a value of 411 units, it is being used loosely in this instance as an approximation of an estimate greater than 205.5, but less than 411.

the sound was always perfect. That means he must have heard the music in his mind, or its neurological/chemical equivalent, and adjusted his fingers to a place he had no experience, premature of the actual act of thought. He had no books, no teachers, no practice, and even more unbelievably, no mistakes.

I, on the other axe, had to work for everything. I was a good student. I enjoyed it and became proficient, but it was learned. I found out early on that I needed hours of rehearsals to perform a song well: to make it feel natural and interesting to my listeners and myself. Quite often, during the learning process, I would find a point I actually became sickened by the mere thought of the piece. The continuous repetition made me question the reason I selected the tune in the first place. I began hating the song, but I kept on, over and over. I found this feeling was usually only a temporary state of mind from simply having repeated it so many times. Only when the mechanics of the piece were truly and firmly embedded in my hard drive, and I played the song before an audience, did the original beauty of the music return. I'd be sittin' there on stage and somewhere in the first chorus, my brain would squeeze out a little drop of honey and my subconscious would go, "Oh, yeah." And once it was in there, it was there for the duration. I feel confident that, even now, I could remember every song I ever performed. We're talkin' maybe four hundred tunes here folks, not too bad for a guy that has trouble remembering to unzip before he pees.

I also discovered it was best for all concerned and the public at large if I stayed close to the beginning of the fretboard. Everything went much more smoothly if I stayed the other side of the fifth fret. I was a great rhythm guitarist and nothing more. There was no flash, no custom paint job. I was just a rock: a nice, medium-sized, dense, smooth rock, and that's not all that bad (Oh, remind me to tell you about Rusty at some point during this story).

Mike had fire arcing from his fingers and was known for his ability on the guitar. Often, audience members were warned to don protective glasses for their own safety.

I never gave any listener any reason to listen too closely to mine. It was just there and it did its job. The end result was that we both appeared competent.

Our voices, likewise, had their own unique pros and cons. Mine was rich and inflective, full of warmth and emotion. Mike's sounded like an old tractor at the beginning of spring. Thank God the boy got shit for vocal cords, or Sinatra would have been driving a forklift in some warehouse in New Jersey.

Now here's the kicker in this part of the contest: although the quality of his vocals was never quite as smooth or even as a broccoli and beer fart, nobody could sing better. He never wavered and he never faltered. He could sing a song correctly on the first try. He could memorize lyrics after hearing the song once, and he could sing any harmony part immediately. So we were still kinda tied.

There is a thing called stage presence or charisma that enters into the equation for people foolish enough to pursue the performing arts as a livelihood. Mike and I were like clones. We both were funny, witty, and really fast. We both loved hecklers and unplanned events for the opportunity it provided us to improvise. In this case though, my trait was natural and Mike had to work for it, or steal it. I mean, he had learned a line or comeback for every possible situation. I remember when an airliner full of people crashed through the roof and killed almost everybody in the place. Mike wryly tipped his hat and retorted slyly, "Thanks for droppin' in folks. I knew that one would just kill ya." Man, I laughed till I cried. He must have been saving that one for years! Only a few waitresses might have ever noticed he had repeated a jab or remark previously. I was better at this, but only we two knew.[3]

---

[3]Mike, you did know I was funnier than you were, right?

We had our own personas and they both worked well. Mike was a loud, animated, fraternity party. I was more laid back and cool.

So, really the only difference to the average drunk was our physical appearance. I've never been one to toot my own horn, but I got screwed on this one. I mean, just look at me, I'm beautiful, right? Tall, thin, blonde, and incredibly handsome. I was a Nazi's wet dream (hang with me for a minute would ya, the part about Rusty is coming up pretty soon now).

Mike was okay, I guess. I mean he was no "me," but at least the poor guy tried. Sure, he was big and strong, and I guess there are those that like that type. Basically, everything would appear to be pretty much even-steven.

As the weeks passed, Mike and I became aware of an interesting phenomenon. We found that on our respective performing nights, the one of us who had the stage had much more luck with the females.

Now we found this weird because nothing else had changed. On Monday night, for example, I'd play and Mike was almost always at the bar. We found no matter how lucky the other had been the night before, on their off night they couldn't make eye contact with a potato.

So, if you were on stage you got paid AND laid. If you were at the bar that night, the chances of romance were slight.

It's utterly amazing how much more attractive a guitar can make you. Although, in your case my dear reader, you might want to consider getting two.

It was at this stage of my life that I met Rusty.

2

I was living with my parents in Dallas and attending classes at one of the community colleges, taking music and theater courses. It was at Richland College that I first ran into Rusty. I was maybe nineteen and he was about twenty-two or so.

I saw him sitting in one of my theater classes. We were all sitting around in a circle in a basement theater. I didn't like a damn thing about him. He dressed nice, had long, straight, blonde hair and was obviously trying to steal "my look" (I knew I should have patented it when I had the chance).

I glanced at him when he wasn't looking, and a couple of times I caught him looking at me. I knew he was going to be tough competition. I'm sure he must have felt that he had no future left after seeing me. I mean, I was after all, you know, beautiful and everything.

As fate would have it, we got stuck together in a project and had to cooperate. I found out he was extremely funny and I had a hard time keeping up my hate for him.

One night, we all went to a pizza place and he and I sat next to each other. He drank beer well, almost as masterfully as I did. I knew immediately he'd had previous experience in the field. He, likewise, must have sensed my expertise with a mug, as a mutual truce was called while we sorted out the details.

I, as always, was willing to try. I'd do my part if for no other reason than for world peace and all that other crap. I set forth my terms for an alliance.

As long as Rusty was willing to accept, unconditionally, the fact that I was his superior in looks, humor, talent, and coolness, I would uphold my end of the agreement. He, in turn, was awarded dominance in the categories of hair, clothes, and experience. I could have contested hair, but I let it slide for the moment. I figured I'd give him the opportunity to concede and save face graciously.

I later found out that he drove a hot rod pickup truck and that was pretty neat. He lived on a small ranch out in the country (another score). When I first met him, he had a live-in girlfriend. She was hot and pretty sharp, so I had to get rid of her. Once she was gone, we were free to explore the Dallas nightlife.

Rusty and I found a small, crowded bar named Bully's and moved in. We had a permanent bartender and I spent most nights out at the ranch. Things were going well. The girls in our classes were mostly freshmen and would fall for just about anything, and I found Rusty to be a great weaver of the fabric of bullshit. We became inseparable.

One morning at Richland, Rusty came out of a door as I was trying to enter. We froze and looked at each other. We both were wearing tight jeans, black boots, a belt, and a vest. Both of us had perfectly starched white, long sleeve shirts. We both had a gold chain around our necks.

"You dumbass," Rusty said.

"Man, what are we gonna do?" I asked frantically.

Rusty stared at me and then shook his head. "Okay, I got my blue jacket in the truck."

"Okay," I said, relieved. I'm sure nobody but us ever noticed this event. Everybody always confused the two of us anyway, but still, we didn't want it known that we were really the same person.

Once we traveled to New York to see some shows at Thanksgiving. New York bars, back then, were great. They were sophisticated and dangerous. It was cool.

Somewhere around this time I was discovered.

A friend of a friend wanted to go into the music management business. This guy, Bill, had watched me for several years as an entertainer and a songwriter, and approached me with an offer. I was like maybe twenty-two or so. We talked things over for several weeks and came to an agreement. We set up the company, with me serving as an owner and a client, and we hired our friends to work for us. Rusty knew sound and lighting equipment, so he became our sound and lighting tech. We hired a band and roadies. We bought tour buses, rehearsal studios, trucks, limousines, custom clothing, stage equipment, and flashy jewelry. And, unfortunately, lots of cocaine.

I've never been into drugs much, but the cocaine affected me. It affected the whole operation. Half of us were reasonably straight and the other half were wired all the time.

We traveled, had lots of women, and other exotic things. It was all free and not totally a bad way to live, if you didn't mind dying at thirty. Someone's got to do it, right?

We were a rowdy, showy lot and we always made a scene. We owned the place — well, we rented it anyway.

We were actually ordered to leave the state of Idaho. Can you believe it? The whole state! We were escorted to the border by the local sheriff and the state police. I was so proud.

It wasn't a total waste of time and resources though. I did manage to learn a few things along the way. For example: in chemistry, did you know that if you mix ANYTHING with cocaine you get shit? It's the truth. Trust me.

We kept it going for a year and a half or so. Finally, things started showing signs of structural weaknesses.

Our bankers stopped coming by for a snort and a whore, and began to start getting their asses into hot water with their institutions. Wives and girlfriends started receiving phone calls that upset them, and lawyers started entering into the picture. Everybody started looking for the money, but there was none. It all became very nasty as everybody grabbed whatever they could and headed for points beyond.

Some of the guys that were financially liable stayed hidden for over ten years. Rusty and I went back to school.

Rusty's father was an accountant specializing in the hiding of cash for nightclubs and restaurants. He must have been very good at it, because he had an impressive list of clients. The average person would have known a few names on this list. Some of the names I knew were of questionable character. Now I don't claim to understand finance and I don't really know how this next wonderful thing happened, but somehow Rusty's father ended up with a small string of topless clubs in his name. The actual ownership was never really revealed, but from time to time, slick, scary guys you wouldn't want to mess around with would drop in and visit the back office. Occasionally, they would drop into the girls' dressing rooms.

Rusty became the manager of several of these clubs. It was incredible. It was probably about this time that I began to believe, indeed, there was a God and he had chosen me above all others. I don't know if you've ever had a harem of beautiful, enthusiastic women before, but it's not all that bad.

Rusty got rid of the ranch and bought a nice four-bedroom condo with a maid. I played happy hour at one of Rusty's places and it really cut into my social life. I remember having to leave pool orgies right as they began to get going. Or, worse yet, I'd have to rise from bed before three. Sometimes the sun was still shining, for Christ's sake, but I persevered for the sake of the organization. I guess we all had to do our part, you know?

I occasionally would watch the door, take the cover charge and check IDs, or bartend. Both jobs were great because you could steal money at either position. Rusty didn't mind and even expected it as long as you didn't steal too much. He always seemed to have enough left over to pay for our carousing. Things continued like this for a year or two and it became our way of life.

One night Rusty and I were sittin' at the bar and he said, "We need a vacation."

I agreed.

"You wanna go to Galveston for a couple of days?" he asked.

I shook my head. "I don't know if I can get the time off," I moaned.

Late that night we had the bartenders load up Rusty's T-Bird with a case of Jack Daniel's, six or seven cases of beer, an ice chest, and a case of good cabernet. We dumped the contents of both cash registers in a paper bag and bid farewell to the staff. They didn't mind our leaving; they knew while we were gone they could steal even more money than usual. It's what is known in the business world as a "win-win situation."

On the way out the door, one of the dancers, Bambi, or Summer, or something like that, asked, "Can I go?"

Surprisingly, we hadn't even thought about that aspect of our trip. I guess we had just assumed we would graze locally while we were there.

I looked at Rusty, he at me. He shrugged his shoulders. "Sure, come on."

Now, this girl Bambi (or whatever) was somewhat new to the club. She was petite and very pretty. She was young and perhaps a bit naïve. Her hair was dark brown and she wore it parted on one side. She was outgoing and friendly. She might have even had some real dance training in her youth. She could have passed, to the untrained eye, as normal.

Rusty, Bambi, and I all took a few valiums to help relax us for the trip. We opened a bottle of wine and headed south down Interstate 45. As the sun rose, we flew through Houston and everything was well on Earth and in Heaven.

We arrived in Galveston around eight o'clock in the morning, a little wasted and weary. We went to the Hotel Galvez, which was a fine old hotel, and crashed like zombies. The hotel had blackout shades on the insides of the drapes, so we creatures of the night felt right at home. We slept all day.

Around six that evening, I heard Rusty and April (or whatever her name was) begin to stir. I heard the comforting spew of cold beer cans being opened. Rusty opened the shades slightly and we could see the lights of the clubs and restaurants along the beach begin to shine dimly. Rusty called for room service and ordered a large breakfast of everything on the menu.

We had a drink and ate breakfast. We showered and dressed for the evening. Amber (or whatever) wanted to go swimming in the ocean. Rusty said he would walk her down to the beach and we would meet at the club in the Holiday Inn in a few hours. I dressed and strolled along the seawall that runs the length of the beach. The clubs were hopping and the lights were inviting. I stopped in a few places along the way for a sip. It was a warm, clear night and you could hear the waves rolling in one after another in the darkness below the stars.

3[4]

I eventually made my way alone to the bar at the Holiday Inn. It was around eleven o'clock and I wasn't thrilled with the place too much. It was a glitter and glass discothèque with a bunch of young college kids that all seemed to know each other. I sat and had a drink or two and waited for Rusty and Amber to show, but they never made it. Around one o'clock, I headed back to the room, thinking they might have retired earlier than originally planned. Back at the Galvez, there was no sign that they had been around. I grabbed a beer from the cooler and stretched out on a bed. I was dozing fully dressed when Rusty burst in the front door. His eyes were as large as golf balls and they bulged out of their sockets. The parts that were supposed to be white were blood red and his pupils were dilated. He was blanched white and shaking noticeably.

---

[4]In 1900, Galveston, Texas, was hit by a devastating hurricane. Tidal waves and flooding killed as many as eight thousand people. That's more souls lost than in the Johnstown flood in Pennsylvania and the San Francisco earthquake combined. Back then, they had no seawall. The beach tapered up from the gulf to the long boulevard that runs along the coastline. After the tragedy, the citizens added this huge concrete barrier to protect the city from the angry sea. They actually raised the whole city seventeen feet. The seawall appears from street level as a large wide

"I think she's dead, man," he shouted.

"What? Who's dead?" I asked, sitting up.

"That girl Bambi, or whatever."

I jumped up. "What happened?"

Rusty stood dumbfounded and trembling. "She flew off the seawall."

"What?"

"She just jumped," he repeated. "She flew into the air."

I got up in his face. "Rusty, where is she? Is she in the hospital?"

He shook his head. "I didn't know what to do. She disappeared into the air." He was terrified. "I didn't know what to do. What should we do? Should we get outta here?"

I grabbed him. "Rusty, where is she?"

He looked me in the eye. "She's in those rocks down below. I couldn't see her in the dark. She wouldn't answer when I called. I think she's dead, man."

"Did you call the police?" I asked.

He shook his head. "I didn't know what to do. I just ran here."

I sprinted down the hall, out into the street, and looked along the long walkway across the street. Further beyond, I could see faint, white curls of water rolling in.

"Where were you, Rusty?"

He was close to crying; he pointed to a spot about a block away. "Somewhere down there." I went running down the center of the boulevard towards the seawall. There were not many cars out and I wanted to attract attention. Rusty walked behind me, following on the commercial side of the street.

---

strand or walkway. On the seaward side it drops off to the beach below. It's a seventeen-foot sheer drop down to the beach from the seawall and walkway. It's seven miles long. In addition, engineers have piled up large blocks of granite at the base of the wall to help break the waves and to reduce erosion. These blocks are approximately one cubic yard with sharp points and were dropped randomly. This was done to break up the

A cop car passed me going the other way and I flagged him. They did a U-turn and pulled up behind me with their spotlight shining on me. I kept running. They pulled up next to me and the cop in the passenger seat rolled down his window and shouted, "What's your problem, man?"

I pointed as I ran. "A girl fell off the wall over there."

"Oh, shit!" the cop said, and then sped ahead of me. They jumped the curb onto the wide walkway and slammed on their brakes. One jumped out with his flashlight and the other was on the radio.

It was hard to see among the rocks below, even with a flashlight. There were so many crags and large voids in the blocks, holes large enough to easily conceal a small woman. I found a place where I could see some sand below me. I hung from the concrete wall and dropped down the remaining eight or nine feet.

Rusty was at the top of the seawall, crying in that cute drug and alcohol induced way of his. The cop on the wall walked along slowly, lighting up the rocks below him. I climbed over the blocks listening for sounds, or trying to make out any shape other than stone. It was extremely dark and all lights from the drag were blocked out by the wall. Just over my head, focusing their beams somewhere out in the gulf, were the cops.

"I think she's over here," the cop above me shouted and held his light steady. I could hear other emergency units arriving up on the street. I climbed between two blocks and found her wedged between them. She was twisted in an odd angle and she was bleeding in several places. I reached down and took her hand; she moaned softly.

"Can you hear me?" I asked quietly. She moaned again. I

---

force and momentum of any dangerous swells. Bathers and others wanting access must enter the beach area down concrete stairs inset into the seawall. There are many of these sets of steps and they're every few hundred feet along the boulevard and seawall. It's a little bit of a hassle, I guess, but the locals find it's much easier than trying to breathe underwater.

crawled the few feet back to the wall face and looked up at the cop. "She's still alive," I said, not wanting her to hear me.

He shook his head in disbelief. "Wow."

Not that there was a *good* place, but poor Bambi couldn't have jumped off the seawall in a worse place. She was equally between two of the descending stairwells that led to the beach. Either way, the rescue workers had a long way to go through the deep sand and blocks of granite to get to her and get her out. It became pretty crowded down there, so I walked up the steps and returned to where Rusty and the cop were talking. Rusty was still shaking uncontrollably, but he didn't seem quite so freaked out.

"What happened?" I asked him, and he laughed nervously.

"Man, we left one of those bars over there," he said, pointing over his shoulder, "and she was pretty loaded." He paused, took a deep breath, and continued, "I guess she didn't know. It was really dark. She saw the ocean and started running. I was in the middle of the street when it dawned on me she might not know the sidewalk dropped off like a cliff." He shook his head. "I shouted, but she ran and leapt on that park bench and did some kinda ballet thing in the air." He looked up at the cop, then at me. "She just kinda held there in space for a second with her arms out like she was posing or something then — whoosh, she was gone."

"Well, she's damn lucky to be alive," the cop said, and then he asked, "What's her name?"

Rusty and I just kinda stood there acting real stupid and deaf. What should we have said?

"Hell, we don't know. Just call her Brandy or Amber or something like that," one of us finally said. So the rescue guys took poor April (or whatever) away, Rusty and I went back to the room, had a beer, and watched the sun come up over the pool out in the courtyard. It had been a nice day.

We woke up about four o'clock the next afternoon, got dressed, and went to the hospital to check on the damage. She was pretty much out of it. The doctor told us she had a compound fracture in her leg, a broken wrist, and several broken and cracked ribs.

She also had a number of cuts that required stitches. She was pretty well mangled and we knew she was probably not going to be much use to us for the rest of our vacation.

We retreated to a nice little bar to consider our options. We were running a little low on cash and desperately low on women. It was decided that I'd head back to base camp for provisions.

Dallas was only about five hours away and it wasn't quite seven o'clock, so I could easily get there before the bar closed. I wore my blue, seersucker cotton drawstring pants with a matching vest, sandals, and no shirt. Rusty filled up my goat skin wine flask with a really good burgundy and placed the strap over my head, reminiscent of a scene from *Flight of the Phoenix*. We said our goodbyes. I gassed up the T-Bird and took off, leaving Rusty sitting at the Hotel Galvez lobby bar.

I got to Dallas in four and a half hours and the bar was swinging. I loaded up a few bottles of liquor, refilled my wine flask, and emptied both cash registers into a paper sack. Then I sat back and had a drink or two with a few of the girls.

By closing time, I had convinced Eva and Lisa that they needed a few days off at the coast. We piled all their stuff[5] in the car and headed there. We thought it might be nice if we took a valium to help us relax on the long trip. I was very fortunate back in those days to have a physician who was sympathetic to my special needs. I can't begin to tell you how deeply upset I was when he was sent to prison.

Rusty's car was an absolute rocket ship. It could cruise at a hundred and thirty like it was nothin'. I was a little

---

[5]Strippers always carry several days worth of clothing in their big bags — handy for impromptu overnights. Pretty smart, huh?

tired though and had my passengers' safety foremost in my thoughts. I kept it around 116.

When I first saw the highway patrol car lights, I was just outside the city limits of a town named Madisonville. It was about five in the morning. I pulled over to the side of the road immediately, exited from the car, and stood politely and patiently for the officer. I'm sure he was running the plates on Rusty's car, and God only knew what that might have meant. For just a moment, I thought I foresaw the fall of the roaming empire.

He strolled up to the car and did a double take when he noticed my goat bladder wine flask that was draped around my neck. Over the course of the last twenty hours or so, I had missed my mouth on a few occasions and the front of my cotton vest was soaked and encrusted with purple stains. You probably could have sucked on it and gotten a nice little buzz. I'd have to remember to be sure and tell Eva and Lisa about that.

I think the cop was pretty cool or maybe just dumbfounded at such an unusual sight. You know, truthfully, if our roles had been reversed, he'd still be in jail and I would have left law enforcement to work in a topless club.

He told me the chase had begun miles back in a town called Centerville. I had been flying so fast and had such a lead on him that he couldn't catch up till Madisonville. He said he'd been chasing me for thirty minutes. I think he was a little proud of himself and I congratulated him.

Yeah, he knew that was wine in my goatskin. Yes, he saw all the alcohol in the trunk. He found the big sack of money too. He noticed the 'script of 10 mg Valiums in the glove compartment next to the Smith and Wesson .38, and I think he even noted the fact that there were two naked women in the car.

I've always been able to hold my liquor pretty well, so in that regard, I felt I was pretty safe. (Even back then they took the "drinkin' and drivin'" thing kinda serious — you had to be able to stay on the road and stuff like that, but it was still acceptable in court proceedings to use the "how was I supposed to know I was driving reckless, Your Honor, I was plastered" defense.)

I was respectful and cooperative, 'cause we all know if he had wanted to, he could have busted me forever and ever.

In the end, he told me not to drink anymore tonight and told the girls they didn't have to put on their tops as long as they stayed in the car. I got a ticket for doing 116 mph in a construction zone marked at 40 mph.

Of course, I had no intention of paying any ticket. What were they going to do, come to Dallas and find me? I worked for cash only. Nobody knew where I lived — hell I didn't even know where I lived. There was no mailing address.

God, I love Texas.

4

The sun was coming up as we pulled into Galveston. The girls were flagging and flashing, sagging, and fagging by then and had run out of fun. We went to the room, found a bed, and folded thee ol' hands.

The next afternoon when we awoke, Rusty showed delight in my selection of companions. Both girls were very nice and both were very attractive. One could almost describe them as interchangeable.

We went to a store and bought picnic supplies, plastic rafts, and other toys before we went to the beach across the street from the hotel. After lunch, Rusty and Lisa went for a long walk along the beach while Eva and I blew up the rafts and went for a swim.

The water was warm and clear. We floated out way beyond the point of common sense. I had tied a small ice chest between the two rafts and had, in effect, made a white trash recreational watercraft — and as white trash are wont to do, we laid about in our slothful ignorance and became shamefully intoxicated. Forgive me 'o brothers, but one thing led to another and somehow Eva and I came to the general conclusion that we were all alone in the world. Surely, we argued, no one could see us at this distance with any hope of resolute detail. So we did as our drunken forefathers had done and discarded our meager apparel. It really seemed like the appropriate thing to do at the time. We climbed aboard the same raft and placed our swimsuits atop the ice chest. All we needed was a television with a broken channel changer knob.

To this day, I don't know the precise details from the land side, but it has now come to be my understanding that there are people on many beaches known as lifeguards. And among the wide array of modern tools at their disposal was an optical device known back then as binoculars. Not only did the lifeguards have these instruments, but a number of the beach crowd had similar viewing devices. These binoculars have the almost magical ability of making far away entities appear much closer than they are in reality. One could see great details at unusually great distances.

It started off with a lifeguard waving at us enthusiastically. I saw Rusty standing next to him and I could tell by his movements that he was laughing and egging the guy on. Eva and I waved to let them know we were okay and that they should just go on about their business.

A fat, little, adolescent boy joined the small group on the beach. Then a young mother began pointing at us and then began shaking her fist at the lifeguard. The crowd began to grow larger as the lifeguard blew a whistle, which we couldn't hear, though everybody on the beach sure seemed to be able to.

There was a restaurant/bar that extended out into the gulf on large poles. At the end of this pier establishment, diners and drinkers alike began to migrate to our side of the patio. They leaned on the rails and made rude noises and held their cocktail glasses up in the air.

We decided maybe we should don our swimsuits and try to bullshit our way out of this. I handed Eva her bikini that had been on the ice chest and turned back for my shorts. They were gone. I looked around our flotilla desperately and, for an instant, I thought I saw my shorts just under the surface of a swell a few yards away. I watched the area for some time, but they never reappeared.

Eva didn't seem to be worried about it too much — but then, she had clothes on.

As the situation sadly progressed, we (I) began negotiations with the grinning lifeguard and his mirthful band of land-loving troublemakers. Rusty was their cheerleader. He danced before them laughing, and incited them with mischief. I saw the two Galveston cops from a few nights previous sitting on the top of the seawall with large smiles on their faces.

I grabbed the tethered plastic rafts and pulled them up around my chest as I neared the shore. I kept my lower torso beneath the water level. The lifeguard was adamant in his request that I come to him. I yelled to him that I think a wave might have pulled my swimsuit off accidentally.

"Oh, we noticed," he said, laughing. "Now come on up here."

I swear that there were two hundred people standing on the beach laughing as I left the water dragging those stupid rafts and ice chest. I looked around for Eva and noticed she had exited further down the beach and seemed to have little or no interest in talking with the lifeguard and his merry men.

Rusty came running down to the water and began jumping about and shouting, "Man, everyone on the beach could see you guys! Didn't you see us waving, you dumbass?"

I'm sure I was blushing profusely as I came up to the lifeguard and I felt the crowd gather around me in a horseshoe.

He smiled and took out a notepad. "May I see some identification please?"

I just stood there looking like a Delbert with my little friend Willie. "You're kidding, right?"

He gave me the longest three-minute lecture ever delivered in front of anyone in the Northern Hemisphere, and then finally let me go. No towel, no clothing, just my pink and yellow plastic rafts.

Everyone made catcalls as I exited the beach and made my way past the throngs of traffic that had stopped up on the street. Horns honked, people yelled, and snapped pictures. I walked across the street and down the sidewalk past the packed bars and restaurants to the hotel. The doorman kept a straight face as he opened the door for me.

Later that night, by my request, we had room service and drinks in the room and on the patio. Somehow I ended up with Lisa as my date. We sat out by the pool a little and stayed pretty close to the room. Just as the evening was getting a little cozy, the phone rang and Rusty answered it. It was Amber (or whatever). She was being released and wanted to know if we could pick her up at the hospital, so Rusty drove down to pick her up.

The poor kid had a cast that covered her entire left leg, a small cast on her wrist, and they had her wrapped tight with gauze from below her arms to her waist. She was so loaded with painkillers that she couldn't feel a thing. We offered her a drink and she offered us some of her medication. It was kinda like Thanksgiving in the French Quarter. At bedtime, we couldn't believe she actually wanted to take part in the proceedings, or maybe I should say festivities. What a trooper. I just love to see people that actually take pride in their work. I guess you can't keep a good man down.

I think this is about as far as I want to go with this aspect of my narrative — after all, this was intended to be a children's story.

So, the next day, we loaded up the truck and moved

the whole damn clan back to the Emerald City — shining brightly with hope on the fertile plains of Paradise. It had been a nice vacation, but we were kind of anxious to get back to work. We were probably more at home amongst bartenders and whores. Home was calling.

A few years later Rusty had the brilliant idea of opening up a '50s themed nightclub. The classic film *American Graffiti* had been a smash hit a few years before and the idea was hot. It was an excellent opportunity and Rusty was in on the first wave.

The new club did very well. So did the next one. They did so well that Rusty eventually got rid of the topless clubs and spent all his efforts on these two clubs. The places were packed six nights a week and the money rolled in.

I put together the large house band and it was great. It was the first time that I'd ever had the luxury of experimenting with horn parts. When I wasn't on stage, I'd spin records from the front of a '57 Chevy. It was a nice time in my life.

Not too long after this, I contracted some kind of brain disorder and got married. Rusty continued on and I continued folding laundry. Later on, I started playing music at other places again. I traveled a lot back in those days and I think it was one of the reasons my first marriage lasted so long. Occasionally though, I'd look out in the audience over the next five or six years and see him sitting there making faces or I'd hear somebody yell from the back of the club, "Get off the stage, you fuckin' hack!" and I didn't even have to look up. He could always make me laugh.

Eventually, I heard that Rusty's clubs were sold and then there was less and less news about him. And in that weird, lazy way, a few days became a few decades.

Twenty-five years later on a cold and rainy (or maybe that just sounds better) night, Patti and I stopped by The

Point for a burger. I dropped her off at the front door so she wouldn't have to walk so far in the weather.[6]

After parking the car, I strolled in. Patti was waiting for me in the alcove. The inner door to the club opened and a guy stepped out. He had a large sack of carryout and was walking while he was looking for his keys when he bumped right into Patti. They both laughed. He says to Patti, "I'm sorry darlin', I'm just an old dumbass."

And me, I smiled.

---

[6]Huh, maybe it really *was* raining. You know, at first I was just sayin' that, but I think now it really might have been raining. I don't know why I just don't tell you guys the truth the first time. It'd be a lot easier for both of us.

Kind of an Epilogue

When I first wrote this story, I did as I always do and passed it off to my idiot neighbor Karl. He's a real dipstick (if you know what I mean), but I find him useful as a sounding board for my writing, plus he usually has cigarettes hidden in his cabinet above the microwave. He loves to read and he's one of the few people I know who actually has nothing better to do than read my crap.

He usually likes what I write and finds the funny stuff close to his warped sense of humor. He's such a wimp that the girly emotional stuff gets to him also. Karl is an odd mix of a sharp, quick wit, but with a dull, thick, lead-like quality as well. It's like he catches all the little stupid shit, but misses the big picture, ya know?

Anyway, Karl took his copy and read it. I just took for granted that he would enjoy it. I was surprised and my feelings were hurt when he said he was disappointed in it and it was his least favorite thing I'd ever written.

I thought the story had some good things in it, and my natural instinct, when criticized, is to become defensive and insulting to the critic. Surely, I surmised, I had outgrown Karl's limited imagination and intellect. It must have simply been over his worthless little (balding) head. Wanting to appear concerned and conscientious, I asked Karl, in his humble opinion, what he thought the problem with the story of "Rusty and Me" was.

He said he thought it was lacking in substance and had no real conclusion. It had no moral.

So what? I thought. It didn't have a windshield or a clothespin either, dickweed.

Who'd he think I was, Mark Twang or something? Do I look like one of them Grimm Brothers? Do you see me dancin' around like Danny Kaye singin' about ugly ducklings?

Look, I'm sure I've goosed somebody's mother along the way, but that's the closest I've ever gotten to a fairy tale. Karl, you moron, you want to sit on my lap and have me tell you a story you can understand? You want a cracker to suck on, you little baby?

Okay, okay, let's all just take a deep breath and compose ourselves, alright? Maybe, just maybe, Karl has a point, and being the curious, caring person that I am, I re-read the story with the needs of my "special readers" foremost in my considerations.

I read the story a few times over the course of several days, and I tried to think of something heavy and thought provoking that I could use to tidy up the ending — 'cause Karl thought it needed a moral.

But, try as I might, I could find no correlation between anything heady and my little story. I went through all my standard "smart guy" literature looking for something I could steal. My collection of reference books and notes yielded nothing useful. I tried Churchill, the Bible, Shakespeare, and even Woody Allen, but I couldn't seem to locate anything I could use to make it look like I was naturally profound or enlightened. Nothing had the right feel and, when I tried to force it to fit my needs, it looked like a cheap add-on, and you deserve better than that.

I needed a deep message. After all, I'M THE GUY WHO ACTUALLY READ *THE DEAD SEA SCROLLS!*[7]

Yesterday was a Saturday. Patti and I were sittin' on the couch about eight o'clock in the morning talking, when all of the sudden the Space Shuttle *Columbia* blew up. There

---

[7]True, it took me a couple of years and I did it by accident, but at least I can say I did it. See, I thought it was the new Bill Bryson book; I figured he was just bein' weird or something, now that he's got all that money and stuff. The first year or two I just kept readin' and readin', knowing that the funny stuff was coming up in a page or two. When I finally finished it, I put it down and realized I'd picked up the wrong book!

was a big thud from overhead. We looked at each other, shocked.

"What the hell was that?" she asked me.

Initially, I thought that someone had jumped on our roof. There was another explosion of lesser severity. We sat and listened for more, but another sound never came.

Within the next five minutes, all the news agencies were reporting that NASA had lost communications with the Space Shuttle *Columbia* over Dallas. Its crew had not been heard from in the last four minutes.

We turned on all the televisions in the house to a different channel to see if we could hear anything hopeful or at least encouraging, but they were gone.

I listened to the news reports all day and knew the debris field well. I bet it was weird there, too.

All the networks had all their experts on, spouting their take on the day's events. They all wanted to get to the bottom of this. They all wanted to know answers. How could this happen? What went wrong? They all required a reason. They all wanted to know what the problem was. They all wanted to know WHY?

It bothered me a little to hear such learned people asking such elementary questions. I mean, after all, these were ROCKET SCIENTISTS, but their questions were as innocent and basic as any child's in a grocery store line: "Why?"

Why does something or someone always have to be responsible? And why do we always need to know why? Job got his ass royally chewed just for asking "Why?"

That day, I just kind of walked around the house all day in a funk thinking about the Space Shuttle and how odd it was that, of all the places it could have happened, it happened over our house (and if this event should or would impact the ending of the preceding story).

Classical physics states if you do this or that, you can expect a certain outcome. Quantum mechanics theorizes that nothing can be observed with both certainty and precision, and that left poor Albert Einstein out there all alone, trying to tie it all together — kinda like me.

Maybe little things make a difference, maybe they don't. I don't know, even Albert Einstein didn't seem to know. Maybe even the big things don't make a real difference in the end.

I didn't take a shower that day. I put some water on my hair and just faked it, and, in the evening, I got in the hot tub and drank a beer.

As I sat in the warm swirling water, I spied a small red balloon that had escaped and I wondered silently where it had come from and where it would end up. I watched it float north until it disappeared in the dim light of dusk. I figured that was probably about as good as it was going to get. Maybe it's none of our damn business what goes on in this world.

So Karl, I'm sorry. I don't write fairy tales and I probably never will. Why don't you just shut up and go do something about that raggedy-ass lawn of yours. Now that's something I think we can all understand.

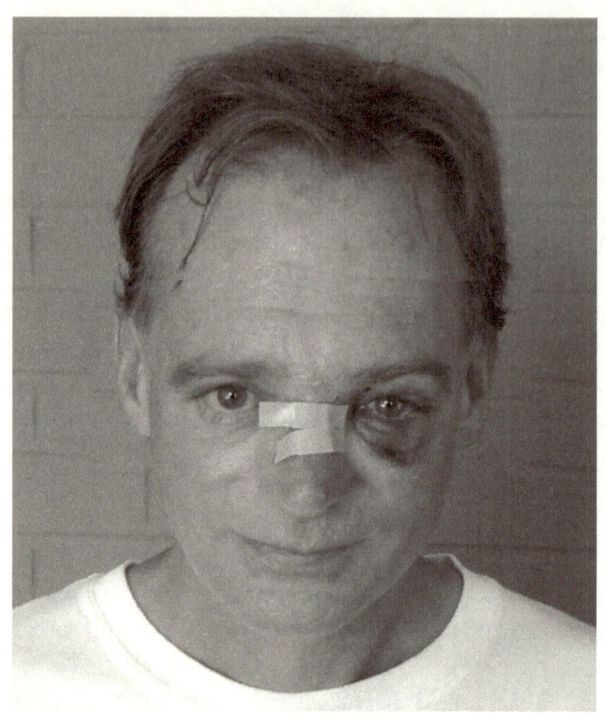

BILLS, BILLS, BILLS

Are you there? I am here. Writing and reading is weird in a way. Isn't this a little unnatural? You and I communicating and one of us could be dead. Here I am talking to someone that I've never met and probably never will. You know, there's *a very good* chance that you don't even exist. At least I won't have to watch you roll your eyes and make that face that tells me you think you might have stumbled into the wrong place or that you accidentally made eye contact with the biggest idiot at the bar.

"Dead Reckoning" is a term that means — well, it means

to forget all that normally makes sense and go with your best instincts. Something told me to write this down. I think it was God that told me to be a writer, but I don't think he ever bothered to mention that I had to be a good one.

Have you ever been hungry? I have, twice: once by circumstance, once by choice. I once went a little over a week without food. I made it by eating anything I could find that wasn't *real* medication in the bathroom cabinet. I tried walking into office buildings, getting off the elevator, walking up to unoccupied office coffee counters and just making myself at home. Almost every office has one. I'd fill the cup up halfway with sugar and milk (if they had it) and add a drop of coffee for effect. Sometimes they had a small box or bowl with small change in it for contributions. I got very adept at making a fake "offering."[1] Once I got a free bagel and I could have gotten a doughnut too, but the lady at the desk was staring at me and I didn't want to risk it.

Here's a perfect example of my standard mind-blowing arrogant pride. Once during this time period I was actually invited out for Chinese and I *had* to say, "No, thanks." I was standing waiting for an elevator and a group of actors and theater types I worked with crowded up around me. "Come on," the director said, "come eat with us."

I was penniless, so I smiled and rubbed my belly and gave 'em the 'ol, "Man, I *just* ate."

The doors opened and they stepped in leaving me standing there. The actor Frank Langella smiled and the director added, "It's on me," while holding the doors open.

I was trapped, I had no choice. If I joined in the feast they'd all know that I was a miserable broke liar (which I'm sure they knew anyway because they were smart and successful), but I waved them off and said, "Maybe some other time." The doors closed forever. To this very day I still can't eat Chinese with Frank Langella.

Have you ever been broke? I don't know if I really ever have been. I've had less money at times than others. I

---

[1] I know what you're wondering and the answer is no, I didn't.

always knew I could find a cigarette *somewhere*, so I figured I could probably make it. I've sat in a cold, dark house with no working phone, but hey, I had a house. I've always been bad with money. When I have it, I give it away. I don't know, I guess it's my guilt. I think we all know I don't deserve anything.

When the Romans were trying to get the "dominating the world thing" off the ground, they kept having problems with these people from Carthage because *they* wanted to rule the world and there was only one world around at the time. The guy with the elephants, Hannibal, was from there. They must have been pretty tough to bust the Romans' chops, right?

It was not so much that each little Roman soldier was a ball of fire, it was more the way they worked *together*. You know, to beat the shit out of everybody and stuff. One thing I find kind of funny and one thing that terrified the Romans as a whole was the bloodthirsty, evil Gauls. The Romans called them barbarians and savages. Just for the record, these barbarians were those skinny white guys from places like Switzerland and Denmark. Woo, I'm so scared. These Gauls (Gaelic) and/or the Celts (Celtic, Seltic, and Keltic) for some reason just made the Romans wet their tunics.

Gauls, by the way, had a weird habit of occasionally fighting naked. Have you ever seen a Dutchman naked? I'm telling you, it looks like a grub worm. Could you imagine swinging a sword willingly against some foe with your shriveled little Johnson poking in the breeze? Twenty-five centuries later when the Germans invaded Denmark, these same warriors said, "You know, you could have just called."

Who were those Carthaginian guys and where the hell is Carthage anyway? I couldn't find them anywhere on the map of Texas, so I sailed to what is current-day Libya on the northern coast of Africa to find out more about these people.[2]

I had to jump ship and swim the last two miles because the Libyans were pissed at us again and the president asked

---

[2]Some of this part is a lie.

me not to go on this adventure as an official member of the
White House Cabinet. Besides, the water there is shallow
and I don't like to get my hair wet.

My old friend Mohmar was waving at me from the
beach as I made my way to the shore. He greeted me in the
traditional Arabian fashion of trying to poke me in the eye
with a hijacked passenger airliner. We both laughed deeply.

"I have a big surprise for you, Richard," Mohmar said
with a beaming smile. (Richard is the long version of his pet
name for me, "Dick.") He grasped my hand and blurted out
like a young girl, "Malcolm is here!" and we both giggled
and splashed, jumping in the sand and surf.

The *real* Malcolm Forbes and I have been close friends
since our days back in Hollywood and we hadn't seen one
another with clothes on in ten years.

Mohmar executed a couple of guys standing near us on
the beach and then we loaded up my luggage and drove to
the palace. It's so cool. He has one of those pink jeeps with
pink and white canvas tops on it — with fringe!

When we pulled into the palace drive, there on the
veranda, I could see the form of my old buddy Malcolm. He
sat astride a vintage '58 Harley. He revved the throttle, spat
on the golden marble beneath his feet and smiled.

"I'll have to clean *that* up," Mohmar chuckled.

After lunch, we three and a bunch of hot Arabian babes
cruised across the desert to one of Malcolm's diamond fields.
We spent the better part of the afternoon running around
picking up diamonds as large as pine cones. Some were even
too big to pick up. The girls had a blast and kept flashing us
their breasts (which is another of their traditional customs).
Finally, we loaded up the diamonds and we headed back to
the palace to party.

I stayed a week (which by the African calendar is twelve
days) and then bid my comrades farewell. I had important
business to attend.

I headed up the coastline in the direction of the Pillars of

Hercules, which is always nice this time of year. I traveled onward, day and night across the vast sea of dunes until I saw a large flashing sign off in the distance that read: "Tunis, Eat Here!" This was the modern day country of Tunisia. Known, I might add, for its blatant rudeness to travelers.

After a large meal of broiled pheasant and a very good

---

[3]Oh hey, one more thing while I've got you here (Have you ever thought that just maybe you might need to get out more?). Once, I was at a big discount center with my kids when they were little. We shopped and bought a bunch of Christmas gifts, you know, like a shopping basket full of stuff. We cruised the slick aisles and were having a nice time being together (Yeah, I'm one of those guys that actually likes shopping). They were at a great age back then, testing the waters of independency, yet sharp enough already to know that their Dad was occasionally — well, you know, full of it. I was proud of their personal growth, their values, and I admired them for being such decent humans, considering their DNA and the crappy cards they'd been dealt in the first few hands.

We looked, felt, and acted as if we were comfortable with the image we were projecting. To the untrained eye, we looked like a nice, normal, loving family. We checked out, loaded the truck, and headed down the road to our place in history.

Later that evening, for some reason, I had a feeling that something wasn't right. There was a painting or possibly a framed photograph somewhere that wasn't hung entirely level. My gears scanned the data forward and back a few times and I became aware of a problem every time I hit the portion that contained the events and entries from the previous daytime hours. I felt a bump as if there was a grain of sand wedged against a magnetic head and it was screwing up all the new information that followed, rubbing a small scratch that slightly infected the current downloads, which really wasn't all that much since, I think, we were watching Lorne Michaels fight for his life with the new season of *Saturday Night Live*. I called NBC and left a message that if he needed a place to crash soon, he could use the couch in the guest room for a few weeks, but then I wanted his sorry ass out. I retrieved the receipt from the T-Mart (or whatever) and skimmed it. It seemed "light" to me, so I grabbed the stuff and began laying it all out on the couch and compared it to the paperwork. Ah-hah, there it was sitting on the throw pillow: the electric razor. It was not itemized on the receipt and was just over a $40.00 error in my favor. The item must not have scanned, but the cashier had removed the magnetic signal that should have sounded an alarm at the door.

The next morning after breakfast I took my kids back to the store to

local white wine, I asked the waitress for directions to Carthage. She looked at me in a way I don't normally allow women to look at me. "What are you, some kinda dumbass or something?"

I immediately left without leaving her a tip. I don't need that kinda shit, ya know?

---

have the razor accounted for. I thought it was very important that they should see firsthand how a person is expected to behave themselves. I took careful aim for them to understand the point, the difference between right and wrong. So I peed in the parking lot and then took them into the store.

The young lady at the customer service center saw a problem coming when she saw us approach her counter and I could see that "oh shit" look in her eyes. I explained that I had made it home the day before with the merchandise in question and had then noticed it hadn't been paid for. I must admit I was a little proud of myself for taking the time to go through all this to help my kids learn a life lesson."I don't understand," she said, "did you steal it?"

"No, no, nothing like that." I laughed with the kids. "Your cashier scanned everything, put it all in bags, and told me how much I owed. Then I paid that amount." She stared with a big ol' gum-chewin' blank.

"So what do you want?" she asked.

Maybe, I thought to myself, this was the first time this young woman had ever experienced honesty for honesty's sake and didn't understand the concept of not trying to get something for free. I don't believe she was trained by her parent(s) to hold such a thing true or dear. So I became even more adamant in my resolve to set an example of pure honesty, so that the same response would not flummox my offspring if by chance they should ever happen upon a noble act.

I thought this kind of stuff was as basic as using a fork with peas or not burping in a nice restaurant. I think maybe this girl's mom had taught her not to throw up on the dining room table or to defecate on the "good" living room rug. "Summer, dammit, don't leave feces on the kitchen counter!"

Before I could answer she cocked her head. "You can't return it."

Before I could check my temper I blurted, "Wanna bet?"

"Not without a receipt," she stated.

I rubbed my head and forced a smile. "Let me speak to your manager."

"Brad, come to customer service please."

Brad walked up smiling. "Can I help you?"

"Yeah, I got this yesterday and they didn't put it on the receipt—"

I took a camel taxi to the airport and flew home later that night. And I'll tell you another thing: I will NEVER go back, so don't even waste your time.

It was either Alexander the Great or the Cowardly Lion from *The Wizard of Oz* that once said, "An army moves on its belly like a reptile." Now, I don't know what

---

"Well," he interrupted, shaking his head negatively, "we can't take it back without—"

"Brad," I interjected, silencing him, "I don't want to return it. I want to pay for it."

He made a weird face, said, "Oh," and walked away.

I paid the $42 and said to my kids, "See," and then the kids and I left.

On the way home we stopped at the grocery store to pick up some food. When we got to the checkout line our total was $42. The kids and I looked at each other.

When we approached the double automatic glass doors they flew open as expected. Right as we began to go outside a wad of green paper flew in. My son picked it up and looked up at me with questioning eyes.

"How much is it?" I asked.

He unfolded it and reported, "Eighty-four dollars. You doubled your money Dad!"

My daughter had a grinning, though eerie, expression.

"Wow," my son concluded. Now I bet a few of you might be thinking, "Oh cool, he got his money back plus his reward." But THAT IS EXACTLY THE POINT of this tale of woe — I HAD to return the money to its owner, or at least try. My kids were shocked. I guess they thought the wheel had gone full circle and I had shown them what was expected of good folks. No, we walked back up to the service counter and returned the money.

I asked the person at the service desk if anyone had inquired about lost cash. They said, "No," and I had them put my name on the envelope containing the money and went home.

Over the course of the next few weeks my kids asked about the found cash constantly. Had I called the store? Had anyone claimed it yet? Can we go to Chuck E. Cheese's tonight? Can we call the grocery store? They were very sharp kids.

Finally after about a month, I called the store. The person on the phone informed me that they had received no found cash and they were sorry about my loss. I loaded up the kids and drove to the store.

The attendant behind the counter once again confirmed that no one had turned in any wayward loot. It was an enjoyable expression on their face when I told them that they were, in so many words, full of shit. And this is not a term I use loosely; I feel most people only contain a small

that means exactly, but I think it means, you know, you *really* should stay in school and not take a lot a drugs and stuff.[3]

What was I talking about? — Oh yeah, Karl, my alcoholic, idiot neighbor.

I sent Karl, my dumb-ass, alcoholic neighbor over to David's house to get one of those tree-cutter-down things.

percentage of shit.

"Really?" I queried dramatically, playing the part of a complete asshole. "We turned in the money. Therefore, we could potentially be having some sort of serious problem with reality and stuff if we can't work this out. This could threaten the whole structure of the universe if we're both right. Just for reference purposes," I asked them in earnest, "what dimension are you in?"

I got the desired response and a few people in line behind us were having a good time. My kids and I love sarcasm. "Look," I explained, "let's just keep this simple. Can you tell me if anyone has claimed the money we found?"

"Yes," she said, lying through her tooth, "they must have, because I don't have it."

"Okay then, now we're getting someplace." I smiled. "Who was it?"

She stiffened and tried to remain cavalier and in control with a big ol' cruel, shit-eating grin. I had her on the run. Right here is the point where you can actually ruin people's lives, by undermining their deepest confidence and psychological infrastructure. It's just a tiny little irritation that rubs against their brain until they finally begin to admit to themselves that they are indeed worthless and they begin to wonder late at night if everyone else knows too. I just love this part. Then I suddenly remembered, this was meant to be a lesson for my children. I could hear God clearing his throat. "Delman," he thundered (using His "little thunder" effect, 'cause it was really not that big a deal), "cut-eth her some slack."

I looked up and waited.

"Please," He finally concluded.

"Ma'am," I said, "let's be honest here, okay? You don't know anything about this subject, so why don't we just start at ground zero. Do you have my money or not?"

She moved her head side-to-side. "You don't have a clue do you? That's okay," I said, quoting Jesus. "Let's just look in the safe and see if we can figure this out, okay? I know this is hard, but I also know that you can do this."

"Okay," she said and turned and pulled open the heavy door.

In a few minutes Karl returned with nothing in his hands but his ever-present beer can. I asked him what was up, you know, like why he had disobeyed me and stuff. He shrugged his little girl-shoulders and shook his head.

"Dude," he said with a startled expression, "David just blew me off man."

Karl waved his hands in the air and repeated, "Just blew me right off — waved me away." Karl's face was red and sweaty and that made his glasses keep sliding down his nose as he jerked about. "Waved me away. Just blew me the hell off."

Man, can you believe it? I couldn't. I don't like it when other guys disrespect *my* Gilligan, ya know?

"What'd he say dude?" I questioned further.

"He had some painter guys over there, ya know?" Karl said and I nodded as I listened.

"No shit!" Karl exclaimed. "He just waved me off with his hand, said 'I gotta pay the painters' and shut the door on me."

"He had to pay the painters?" I repeated.

"Yeah," Karl moaned in disbelief, "said he had to 'pay the painters.'"

And later that night it dawned on me: man, we all gotta pay the painters.

Right there! Right there on the door was a small packet with my name on it!

"Oh," she reached out for the envelope and she handed it to me without another sound. I wondered if people were stupid or just lazy.

A few weeks after we found the first bit o' cash, I caught a cache of cash moving across the parking lot at the same grocery store. This time I bent down, retrieved the bills, stuck them in my shirt pocket without a second thought, got in my truck, and drove away. It's a pretty sad state of affairs when I'm the most honest guy around.

IF DOGS COULD TALK

My friend Mindy (yeah, she's one of my exes) emailed me that her old dog Schotz had finally succumbed to the wishes of the Grim Reaper. I consoled her by quoting from my copy of *The Big Damn Book of Sheer Manliness* by the von Hoffmann Bros., as I always do when I want to sound smart. In it they write: "If there was ever a clear error made by God, evolution, or whatever you choose to call the great determinant, it was the life span of dogs. There's just no logical reason for dogs living as short as they do."

Have you ever thought that maybe dogs were only designed to last about as long as a kid is a kid? Have you ever noticed they're about the same?

Mindy (not her real name, it's Marcia) wrote me back: "True, and I think they should be able to talk, too. By the way, you don't happen to have the money you owe me, do you?"

If dogs could talk, I think the most common thing uttered would be something along the lines of, "Dude, what happened to that cookie I *just* had?"

I returned to my seat after a short bathroom break and addressed Ron and the general assembly. "Gentlemen," I began, "do my eyes deceive me or did I notice a new trash can in the men's room?"

There was a curious look on Ron the bartender's face. The members of the bar turned to one another and whispered. Ron laid his towel down and walked the short corridor to the men's facility and all eyes followed him. He opened the door, stood in the hall, and gazed into the small room. We all watched as he tentatively stepped in. The door slowly closed behind him.

The two blonde guys that always sit on the opposite side of the bar from me (no matter where I sit) stood cautiously, and then they too walked towards the bathroom. They were joined by that dirtbag with the sideburns and the stupid looking mock-leather jacket. This group likewise opened the door and peered in. I could see them speaking to one another momentarily and then they all abandoned the area, returned to the bar, and took their seats.

Ron approached me from behind the bar, took a deep but quick breath, and looked me in the eye. His mouth was tight and his lips moved with a slight nervous jerk. "The guys," he said quietly, "and I... " he paused and looked downward, "think you might be mistaken."

In the shadows I could see them all nodding in agreement.

"Ron," I pleaded, "surely, you're aware that the old trash can was black, right? That trash can in there is blue, man." I continued, but no one spoke in my defense. All eyes were averted downward. I was going to leave without finishing my drink in disgusted protest of their treatment, when it dawned on me that it would really only be hurting me. I decided to ride it out and take the high road for a few minutes, those lying assholes. Someday, I vowed, I would show them. I had already practically written a really good story about the new trash can and everything. (But remember this, my friends: "Revenge is a dessert best served on rye.")

Did you know that at one time I thought about becoming a great poet, as well? The biggest problem was, I couldn't figure out any word to rhyme with "lovin'" except "nubbin," and frankly that just wasn't enough. Plus, back then I didn't know what "nubbin" meant.

But I don't care. I don't care about those lying bastards. I don't care about that kiss-ass Ron. Ya know why, huh?

Because — THE GIRL SCOUT COOKIES CAME TODAY!!

So I stood in the dark kitchen and tried to see just exactly how many boxes of Girl Scout Cookies I could eat without causing permanent damage. I gazed out the west window and saw my neighbor Harry on his porch. Harry lives next door to David. David's okay, but I don't care much for Harry. I think he's some kinda retired golf pro or some useless thing like that. He's pretty much just stale, white bread.

From my position in the darkness I knew he couldn't see me, and there was nothing else of interest going on outside, so I watched him. I could see he was holding his little piece of shit dog in the cradle of his skinny little arm. It was one of those stupid little Pomeranian things that have been outlawed in so many other countries. You know, the little reddish dogs that look kinda like a miniature lion, but more like a sunflower. A GAY SUNFLOWER!

I watched Harry mosey down the walkway leading from his house to the street. He paused and then crossed the silent lane and entered my property. He walked across my west lawn and stopped under the large elm tree. Harry first looked from side to side; he then leaned down and released his pet onto the softness of my newly mowed grass.

Now this was amusing. I wondered to myself what he thought he was getting away with. Was this a kind of reprisal for some long-past or forgotten insult? Was he getting even with me? Was I seeing the criminal dark side of this man ordinarily cleverly disguised as a boring waste of the earth's resources? Was *this* his big act of social defiance? I laughed at this pathetic gesture and the simple nitwit seeking his distilled, all natural, no sugar added, diet-gratification. "Rocks-Lite," I thought and grinned. It dawned on me that we were both getting our cookies.

I'm sad to admit that this was the coolest thing I had seen all week. From my way of thinking, this was quality entertainment. I guess we're both a little pathetic.

Now if that was me, I'd have dropped a dump truck full of elephant dung and then dragged his schoolmarm, pleading wife through the slime in a matching set of black leather bra and garters while their grandchildren screamed like the Romanovs.[1] What'd he think that little Pomeranian was gonna drop? Hell, you could stick that tiny peanut-of-a-thing on a nice sandwich and never even notice it. Go for the gold, Harry, you dumb-ass.

In the 1719 novel *The Life and Strange Surprizing Adventures of Robinson Crusoe,* Daniel Defoe wrote,

> "... and I must not forget that we had in the ship a dog and two cats, of whose eminent history I may have occasion to say something in its place; for I carried both the cats with me, and as for the dog, he jumped out of the ship of himself, and swam on shore to me the day after I went on shore with my first cargo and was a trusty servant to me for many years; I wanted nothing that he could fetch me, nor any company that he could

---

[1]When the executioners of Tsar Nicholas II, his wife, and five children separated the bloody, tangled bodies, they were surprised to find a tiny white dog which was, moments earlier, being held by one of the Tsar's daughters.

make up to me; I only wanted to have him talk to me, but that would not do."

I asked my alcoholic dumb-ass neighbor Karl what a dog might say if one could talk. He thought a minute and then answered, "You know, you guys ain't near as smart as you think you are."

Ya know, a dog ain't nothing really but a wolf with a bred-in haircut that's been fed Alpo for a few thousand years. And just like your kids, if you weren't looking he'd love to get together with a few of his friends and eat a sheep raw.

What do you think it is about us that make us blind to the shortcomings or faults of our pets or even our children for that matter? Everyone thinks his or her own dog is the smartest, the cutest, has the most personality, etc. Why can't people just admit it when their children can't sing worth a damn or they're not all *that* smart?

I wish one of those geneticist guys would find that "numbed" chromosome and put a patch on it. And while you're at it guys, what's the deal with the "genius bone" being connected to the "dumbass bone"? Some of the smartest people I know can't seem to remember to eat (and yes, I'm talking about you).

Now, my dog Comet is a good dog. He's real old and he's a real sweet guy. Kids love him because he's big and fluffy and he will stand there and let you pet him til you're tired. He's obedient, but I don't really know if he's all that smart. Sometimes I just think he wants to please *so* bad that he often appears sharper than he really is. Or maybe, that's what he *wants* me to think.

When I watch him walking sideways nowadays, it's hard to believe that it's the same dog that used to drive me home when I was too drunk.

He brought a pamphlet home from the vet's office the other day and threw it on my desk. The title was "Brain

Aging & Behavioral Changes." I read through it briefly and found one of those "check if symptom applies" games.

"House-soiling," check. "Does not ask to go outside," check. "No longer greets family members," check. "Does not seek attention," check. "Does not recognize familiar people or places," check. "Does not respond to verbal cues," check. "Sleeps more during the day and less at night," check. "Appears lost or confused in the house or yard," check. "Stares into space or at walls," check.

I dropped the paper to the floor. "Oh my God," I thought to myself, "I've got Brain Aging Disease!"

Comet is an Australian sleep-dog. He's deaf now, but he can understand sign language in Texan, English, AND Spanish, and will come for a snack in most Western European dialects. Comet is probably a virgin, and to make matters worse, a latent homosexual virgin. And although I love him, I'm honest enough to admit he can't sing worth a damn.

Comet doesn't bark unless it is time to get your gun or, of course, it is time for the UPS man. I once took him to the large UPS distribution center in Dallas because he got such a charge out of the sounds those brown trucks made. I assumed he'd love it, finding all those trucks with *that* sound, but it terrified him when he saw how many there were. He cowered in the back of the truck until we got safely back home. I don't think before that point in time he understood the global significance and strength of UPS. I believe they view one another now as worthy and respected adversaries. It is, to this day, a delicate balance.

Comet is mostly black, so when you combine that with his deafness and my lack of vision in the dark, there are quite a few reported incidences of trippage in the hallway during mid-night bathroom breaks. I try to yell at him for being so dark-colored but he can't hear me, so we both just limp off in our separate directions groaning. I'm sure someday when we're eighty we'll both be rushed off to the emergency room with broken hips. I want a private room because we both snore and he doesn't like to watch *COPS*.

And speaking of cops, I think you should know that in his youth, Comet had been picked up on charges of tag fraud. He was caught running the streets wearing the valid vaccination tags of a deceased comrade.

Comet used to be a good guard dog, and once woke me up to let me know there was a woman in the house (I think I meant to say, "a duck in the backyard"). Now he's a pressure sensitive warning device (you have to step on him in the dark to activate him).

He looks like an old house shoe, and he sheds so much I don't even really care anymore if he dies. I've got enough hair under the couch to make a whole new dog. I once opened up a fresh peanut I had just purchased at the market — inside I found one of Comet's hairs.

I find it personally embarrassing, and an insult to my family honor, that my daughter Delberina named her new little puppy Bacardi. Now my daughter is still young, so she doesn't know much about taste and sophistication, but that's no excuse for naming a dog after a cheap-ass rum, am I right? See, that's got no class. People in the neighborhood hear you call your dog with a name like that and then *they* know you got no class, too. It's humiliating, 'cause one thing I got for sure is some mother effin' class.

I talked with my daughter as sensitively as I could about possible alternative names for this new smooch pooch.

"You know," I began compassionately, but cleverly planting a subtle seed simultaneously, "the best rum I ever had was called Pussers."

Some comedian that's probably dead now (so I can probably legally steal his stuff) said something like,

"Diamonds are a girl's best friend, but *dogs* are man's best friend — now what kinda deal is that?"[2]

While I was writing this piece, Karl's dog Pasha died. He was seventeen. Karl described his quiet demise in the early morning hours to me. We sat together on his back porch and I listened intently.

"Did he say anything?" I asked at the conclusion of his narrative.

Karl shook his balding head. "No."

I wasn't really expecting too much here because Pasha

---

[2] I think I should take a moment to include the lesser known and underappreciated members of the genus of canines such as dingoes, hyenas, and, of course, the equine family, which includes the adorable miniature donkey.

To learn more about these lovable and valuable cousins of the modern dog, I attended the 2004 National Miniature Donkey Association (NMDA) conference, held semi-annually in Dallas, Texas.

I find it so amusing that many people don't even realize that animals belonging to the equine species (such as zebras, horses, mules, etc.) are really dogs.

I must admit that a few of these facts were completely unknown to even *myself*, until I spoke with one of the participants at the conference.

According to this lady who told me she was a well-known expert, all canines (including those listed above) are born in groups known as litters (which I already knew). Shortly afterwards, they are separated into groups and categorized by a guy in Fort Worth. This man decides which animals are going to be regular dogs and which will grow up to be horses (he has to do the same thing with goats and sheep).

In Dallas, as well as most major centers of international commerce and technology, the miniature donkey provides many important services.

Visitors to Dallas are often surprised and pleased at the site of these little guys moving freely in and out of high-rise buildings, boarding elevators, or just relaxing at Starbucks.

Males are known simply as "jacks" and the females are "jennets," but are also commonly referred to as "jennys."

Miniature donkeys perform a multitude of tasks and important functions, not to mention the many uses to be found for their often sought-after hides. Don't be alarmed here, miniature donkeys are the ONLY ANIMAL IN THE WORLD (besides a few others) that can actually shed their skins completely without causing damage or harm to themselves or others. Some authorities claim they actually enjoy the process!

was a real dip of a dog, and an ass-kisser. He probably would have said something *really* stupid like, "I love cheap, hard candy just as good as chocolate, duh-huh," or, "Kool-Aid in the packet is cheaper than and just as good as premium canned soft drinks." He was always trying to score points with stuff that was just stupid or useless.

"You know Karl," I began, trying to think of just the right words to say to comfort my loyal servant, "I think Pasha was the only dog I've ever heard of that actually scratched on the door when he wanted to come into the house to pee."

Karl nodded quietly in agreement, our gazes drifted to the scarred, fogged, sliding glass door that is standard issue for white trash.

"And you know," I continued, "your wife Pathetica is still pretty hot even if she hates you for the years you've stolen from her." We sat and smoked silently, nodding in solemn reflection. Like I said before, I've *always* had the amazing talent of making people believe I really give a shit.[3]

Anyway, Blackie (my dog before Comet) lived to the age of twenty-two human-years. I found her near downtown

---

[3]Speaking of my limitless talent, you know, sometimes I just feel like letting it all slide, chuckin' it all man. Just glide down the highway to dreamland. I mean it. One day I'll collect my tap shoes and head back to my one true love: dance.

Someday, I'm thinkin' I'll leave the money behind. I'll just forget all the women, press and prestige, and let my feet do my worrying for a while.

You know, at one time, I was considered to be one of the best. Still to this day, there are pockets of people (mostly in the Midwest) that recall my name with a smile. Even after all these years of retirement I can still stop the show when I decide to "strut it." Occasionally, I'll bust a move at a dinner club or a neighborhood street dance. The way people stop and stare, you can just tell they're shocked by my ability. It's almost like they're starved for the simple elegant grace of my talent and genius. The best part is that I never had any formal training. It's a natural gift, kind of like people from Finland, or maybe something even wittier.

when we were both little. She was without challenge the ugliest dog ever to live. She was so short she was barely even there. She was stretched real long, like one of those stupid wiener dogs, but she had a long black wiry coat of hair that almost drug the ground. She had a big ol' moustache like those Scottie dogs. When people would see her they would ask, "What is that?"

"Well," I would begin, "she's a rare European mix. She's half English Wire Backed Terrier, half French Café, and *half* full-blooded Lesser Dane."

"She's a circus dog," I usually added (and I still don't know why). They always just smiled and petted her.

I think Blackie would have asked, "Can we go to McDonald's for some of those chicken nugget things and some of those cheap-ass cookies?"

I think I'm going to keep working on this talking dog thing. I can see some real possibilities.

Thank Jack

If you were to pour a cup of water that was 60° Fahrenheit into an empty bowl and then add another cup of water that is 50° into that same bowl, the two cups combined would become 55°. 'Cause 60+50=110, divided by 2 is 55. Curious? Naw, that's just the way it is. That's life. That's Tuesday night at Chili's. It's what is expected.

And likewise, if you were to pour a cup of water that was 212° into a bowl and then added one that was 33° — it's still the same old thing, kinda. The temperature of the mixed water will be — hold on, I'm mathing here — 122.5°. Each changed 89.5°! That's a huge difference, and that's kinda cool I guess, but still just an average.

So if the last example is similar in theory to the first test, with only a more dramatic difference in the final outcome or average, should it follow that all is to be expected with similar results? Does the equal mix of Part A and Part B always equal an average? If you were to change the last formula by one degree, one critical degree, something weird and unusual occurs. Sometimes, thank God, weird stuff happens.

Let's try the same thing one last time (but with even LESS of a jump in our extremes as the last attempt). This time pour one cup of water at 212° (same as before) into a bowl, but this time pour a cup of water just one degree cooler than last time (32°) into the bowl. The new temperature is 51°! Logic and experience would dictate the new combined temperature to be 122°. This new total is less than half of what should be expected. What made such an unbelievable difference? One degree. You see, sometimes even little things, like one lousy degree, can make a big difference.

Thirty years ago Jack Rumford was a big guy. Even back then he towered over me like an oak, so he must have been a hell of a man because, well, *I'm* a hell of a man. He was maybe six foot seven inches tall, a lean two hundred forty pounds. Jack was a Marine fighter pilot in Vietnam, but I don't think he *really* needed the jet to whup-ass.

He was from Connecticut, but he made his way down to Texas early, took hold, and refused to let go.

I first met Jack down in the Hill Country. He was known for his benevolent sponsorship of the world famous Fredericksburg Bachelors Society. Jack and his girlfriend would hold weekly feasts in which the lowest of the single men of the county, such as yours truly, could be guaranteed to receive, at minimum, a healthy, nutritious meal and a fine glass of wine.

Late into the night we would sit in their small kitchen and listen to stories of humorous deaths and Jack's drunken, violent antics with lesser men. He had a complete library of delightful and deadly narratives. My favorites among these were *Death by Beer Can*, *Oh, I Guess He Wasn't a Spy after All*, and of course the enchanting *The Water Buffalo that Wouldn't Die*.

At that time Jack was officially retired from killing people professionally, but the reminiscences still brought a certain sparkle to his eyes when he had an attentive and intoxicated audience. In the days that I knew him best, he was what we in Texas refer to as "a gentleman rancher." He would drive around in an old truck with a dog in the back and look at sheep and cattle and nod his head a few times. Then he would end up at the Domino Parlor most late afternoons, where he would arrive just in time to pick up the check for our beers; a true American hero.

One curious thing was the fact that Jack didn't drink any longer. He'd given that up a while back when he stopped killing folks. But regardless, whether it was food or drink, Jack picked up the tab. We all figured it wasn't much to him. A few times a month he still flew a route for one of the big airlines from Guam or Hawaii to Australia. We also knew that Jack had a few real estate holdings around town. So we all figured that the money was no big deal to him. He always took care of his friends. That was just Jack.

There was one evening in particular when I thought he was out of town, and I was home alone and depressed. I had not a morsel of food in my pantry and was completely broke. I was feeling down. I planned to take a shower, watch TV, and try and get past it. Then there was a knock at the door of my upstairs garage apartment.

"Why weren't you at the Domino Parlor?" Jack asked through the screen door. "Poor ol' Hoppy had to drink for the both of ya."

"Too broke," I answered as he entered and I headed towards the shower.

Jack came in sporting a new felt hat and looked around my humble apartment. He laid his elbow on top of my refrigerator and leaned against it with his great smile.

"Get dressed and I'll take you out for supper," he said, a little softer and quieter than his usual manner.

"No," I said, shaking my head, "I think I'm in for the night."

"You sure?" he asked, rubbing the brim of his new hat as he held it.

"Yeah, I'm cool." I headed into the bathroom and closed the door. While I was in the shower I heard my battered screen door quietly close and then the familiar sounds of a giant creaking down my outside stairs.

Once I was out of the shower I watched a little TV, and then messed around with my guitar for a while. It was getting late. I walked across my tiny room to get a drink of water. As I filled the glass at the sink I couldn't help but notice a couple of crisp bills sitting on top of my refrigerator. That money was a lifesaver. That was Jack. He was a little different than your average guy.

A couple of weeks ago on a Sunday, I sat and watched a seven or eight-year-old girl who couldn't have weighed seventy pounds as she continuously held her younger and handicapped sister. The younger girl seemed to have a very serious debilitating condition that would not allow her the use of her lower legs, which were withered and malformed. The younger sister was almost the same size as her older sister, but for the better part of half an hour the older girl held and rocked her with patience and with concern. She petted her, stroked her hair, and entertained her crippled sibling. What I found most interesting in this whole affair is that the older girl smiled and giggled and laughed the whole time. She stood there swaying to the music holding her own weight and smiling.

That little girl had more raw strength than any Marine fighter pilot I'll ever know. And she smiled while she did it. It was easy for her. It was a piece of chocolate cake. She was a better person than I'll ever be. No matter what I think I may know or learn, no matter how hard I might try, that little girl will beat me every time in the human race. Some people are better, face it. They're just better than you and I.

Thank God for those that are different. Thank God that there was an Elvis so we can see clearly what an asshole Jerry Lee Lewis is.

There is a difference in some of us; maybe it's even a little thing.

There was a time when the sight of a bum used to piss me off. I considered most of them to be lazy addicts that were too afraid and weak to face life, and you know what, maybe they are: always bothering honest people for a handout, taking the fruits of others' hard-earned labors, asking for my money — like I've asked for others' money.

So I'm tryin', ya know, and it's hard sometimes. Sometimes I forget and have to force myself back on track. Sometimes I have to be shown and sometimes I have to be led back by a little girl.

So nowadays when a bum nervously casts his eyes my way, I just smile and give 'em what I can. After all, it's not mine, it's Jack's.

GRACE AND ELEPHANTS

When my grandfather was first diagnosed with Alzheimer's, my family was, as you might expect, greatly saddened and concerned. What should we do? How should we plan our lives? No one knew for sure. It could be a rapid decline or it could be a lingering illness tainted with bouts of uncharacteristic personality traits or possibly violent or argumentative mood swings. Only the passing of precious time would truly tell.

My maternal grandfather was born in North Texas in early 1900. I don't have much information from his early years. From what I've gathered, nothing extraordinary occurred that should be of major interest.

His name was Virgil Eugene Kelley. My grandmother called him Gene or "Sweets," but we called him Pa.

He married my mother's mother and as a young man in the '30s practiced the trade of blacksmithing in a small corrugated tin shop close to downtown. Of course EVERYTHING was near downtown in Anna, Texas, and the difference between "near" and "far" was measured in feet. His little shop had no insulation and no floor. I feel confident saying that at times the working conditions could have been considered harsh by today's standards.

His sister-in-law (my grandmother's sister Velma) and my great-grandfather had a small mercantile or "general store" a few hundred yards away on Main Street. I remember vividly, as a young boy, going through the swinging screen doors of the store to find the most wonderful assortment of sights and smells. There was candy, ice cold drinks, hats, canned goods, fabric, hardware, apparel, and a thousand other unexpected surprises. My Aunt Velma ran the store alone throughout the '50s and '60s and I always looked forward with excited anticipation to my summer visits.

Sometime during the course of the late '40s, my grandfather switched from his little blacksmith business to carpentry. He built dozens of homes in and around Anna, and quite a few as far away as Dallas. He also built a nice little string of rental houses that my grandparents used to subsidize the income from his labors. This system appeared to have worked pretty well, and he provided amply for his wife, my mother, and her four siblings.

During the years of my youth, he drove his pickup during the workweek. On Saturday mornings he would dust off the seat and escort my grandmother on the four-minute trip to downtown for her shopping. Occasionally, we would drive to Sherman or McKinney for specialized items, or needs, or funerals, but I actually enjoyed the little town's offerings more.

On Sunday mornings, clad in his brown suit and dress hat, my grandfather would open the sacred garage door and back out the ceremonial Chevrolet. My grandmother would stand, poised gracefully, with her sweater draped neatly over her left forearm and clutching her Sunday purse, while my grandfather performed the required duties of the household footman.

Once the Chevrolet was drawn forth, my grandfather would exit the coach and open the passenger door for my waiting grandmother.

If time was short, we would circumnavigate the residence on a gravel road next to the property, cut to the left almost immediately, pass the three houses behind my grandparents' house, head over the railroad tracks, and park in the grass of the churchyard.

But, if adventure called and earthly desires lured its head you could also take the "highway" to Main Street, go over the railroad tracks and park in the grass of the churchyard. This route was my favorite and always made for a scenic and interesting motoring experience, but the extra thirty seconds could be strenuous.

At this beautiful little church, my grandfather taught Sunday school and served as an elder for decades. On Sunday nights we watched *Perry Mason* with the window unit purring softly while the heavy floral curtains swayed slightly against the lacquered knotty pine that lined the perimeter of the large room. My grandfather always carried a sturdy pocket watch in his blue and white bib overalls, along with his hammer and wooden fold-out measuring stick.

Sometimes during the week I would accompany my grandfather on his workday, or sometimes I would stay at the house with my grandmother where I played shirtless and barefoot in her huge flower garden with my cars and trucks and toy soldiers for hours in the blazing Texas sun. The soil of her garden was dead-flat black and so granular it was easily worked into hills, roads, and ravines. It could be poured like water for the purpose of experimentation or even just mindless contemplation.

First, I sold my horse and bought a motorcycle, then a Chevy Malibu, and then — I was grown. I no longer spent my summer with my grandparents. Instead, I listened day and night to AM radio spin the most original music ever recorded. The hot stations in Dallas battled every minute for your audience and the hits kept coming.

Guys in great cars cruised and whistled at girls wearing bikinis. Honda motorcycles sprang up everywhere. I wore burgundy, paisley print, heavy cotton corduroy hiphuggers with a two-inch-wide belt and a polka-dot shirt that had no buttons; it just stayed open in the front. Sometimes I wore sandals, sometimes black suede Spanish high-heel, and ankle-high boots with a zipper on the sides. It was a fashion statement to wear matching colors in your choice of shirt and socks; the more radical the color the better. The guys began to grow their hair out to lengths previously unknown in that century. Everybody owned a guitar and there were a thousand garage bands, each with their own unique gimmick and style. We pushed and changed and changed again. Then there was Woodstock and this brief era began its decline.

Next was plaid, bowties, and pullover sweaters, pleated trousers with loud bold prints for the guys, and long "granny dresses" for the girls. Our bell-bottoms made it through to this new chapter of satirical events unscathed, but only blue denim was considered acceptable. Some of my friends started disappearing into the distant halls of academia, never to be seen or heard from again. The music had a smoother edge and I suspected it would end up having less serious historical value. I was, of course, a little too busy at this juncture in my life to take notice or care. What with guiding and directing the whole Cosmos from my throne next to God, I had no time to consider the daily activities of my grandfather. I don't think my grandfather gave a damn about the current trends in popular music. My grandfather just kept doing his hammer and nails thing quietly, alone in the background.

Shortly thereafter, there came a time when my grandparents were too old to safely make the fifty-mile drive to Dallas without the aid of a driver. I don't think I thought much about them during this point in my life either.

The large circle of friends I had associated with from my boyhood years had withered and dissipated into a tiny group of casual phone calls and periodic rendezvous. I was now alone in the world without the protection of biased insulation I had shared with these people. I made my way forward, defenseless and ignorant into the darkness of the future.

Somewhere during this phase of self-centered isolation, it was announced that my grandfather was ill, never to return to the vigorous sharpness of youth. I was unmoved at this news and didn't really care. It was a part of life, just not a part of *my* life.

The little town of Anna had all but fallen into the dust by this time. Its population had literally died off without replacements from its reserves. The once-bustling stores and shops on Main Street closed up one by one, never to function as a gathering place for local news and gossip again. Never again would they be the platforms and rallying points for polite and friendly exchanges between life-long friends and relatives. Never would they be the pleasant memory of another child, but I didn't care.

My grandfather began to show signs of structural weakness with a fair amount of slippage and forgetfulness, which later stumbled into uncontrolled mental drifting. In the beginning there were tears among those with souls and many an hour of anxious fretting over the blow to personal pride and dignity that Alzheimer's patients must endure. You live a good, honest, decent life only to exit as a blathering imbecile. It is a shame, and I remember vividly thinking at the time that God, in his infinite wisdom, should consider curing this for his pals that have always done right by him.

The family began to note very small changes in my grandfather's behavior and personal mannerisms. He became more open, outgoing, childlike, and friendlier. Gone was his stalwart reserve and conservative wallpaper. I don't think that he remembered he was a married man with grown children and grandchildren of his own, for he flirted innocently with the ladies at gatherings of kith and kin. I must admit that some of his cute antics were so adorable that occasionally a smile would grow and for a few moments his disease wasn't, maybe, all that bad. In many ways, I think he was having a good time dancing to the music and playing with his toys in the garden of his mind. His old pocket watch was now only a confusing bit of silliness. It was as if none of that stuff had ever mattered.

His socks began to become bothersome. They didn't cooperate fully with his plan. He needed to straighten them. He needed to pull them up properly. They should be even and straight. They should behave as good socks should.

My grandfather would sit for great lengths of time and contemplate the troublesome dilemma at hand. He sat and stared at his socks, bending occasionally as if he had finally found the solution: to push them both down until they met the tops of his shoes and then raise them properly with the knitted fabric lines and patterns straight. The tops needed to be perfectly even and straight, like they should be.

It was impossible not to see the humor in my poor grandfather's situation. Not out of anything but love would my aunts ask him entertaining questions about his perplexing state.

"What should we do about these bad socks, Daddy?" a jovial Aunt Pat would ask.

"I think I've figured it out," he'd reply in all seriousness, "they need to be straight and even."

"Maybe you should straighten them," was always sound advice. At once he would lean forward, as my grandmother rolled her eyes, and commence to his task. And you know what? Your socks *should* be straight and even.

It was Christmastime and we were all at my parents'

house. Torn colored wrapping paper littered the floor in heaps and piles, and all my family was together. A splendid fire cracked and flickered. Children ran to and fro, laughing and playing. It was upon this occasion that our lives changed forever.

As we chatted and snacked, I could not help but notice that my grandfather, seated across the room, had begun a new round of "fix the socks." I shook my head and sat holding both of my small, sleepy children in my cradled arms.

"What's wrong, Pa, something wrong with your socks?" some courteous bystander asked him.

"Yes," he stated, "there is a problem with my socks. Do you see how they're not straight? And the tops of my socks are uneven."

My Aunt Mody overheard this exchange from the kitchen and put down her dishtowel. She entered the dining room quickly. Now, you must know that my Aunt Mogene was an exceptionally proper woman and it is important for you to realize that her next statement was completely out of character for her "formal" nature. We sat stunned and were all shocked to the point of silence once she said, "Daddy, why don't you take off your socks?"

My grandfather looked directly into her eyes and didn't say a word.

Slowly he lowered his head and his gaze to the skinny little legs and ankles beneath his seated form. He studied them closely and once he had worked out the math and logistics in his faltering mind, began the hardest task of his life.

In the silent room, without help or aid in any way, my grandfather removed his right shoe and set it neatly aside. Then, even more swiftly and confidently, he did the same with the other. He looked up at all of us with modest pride, but also with a touch of nervousness, and then back down to his stockinged feet.

He reached out and took the top of his right sock, waited for an instant, and then pushed it down and over his heel. Then he grabbed the flopping toe and ripped it off. Then he dropped it to the floor, never to serve its evil upon him again. The other, he pulled off in a rapid, one-tug movement that few have ever completed without mishap.

My grandfather sat with his bare, naked feet exposed to the carpet (and the world) with no shame and no guilt. He was a man. The room returned slowly back to its prior mood of festive mirth and merriment, but it was not the end of my grandfather's rebirth. In just a few minutes the children began to slide back into game mode and the volume increased. Adults began to talk quietly again and everything appeared normal and right. I watched Pa in his chair. He curled his toes into the thick carpeting and slid them back and forth in a relaxing manner; his aged eyes never leaving his newfound feet.

Suddenly the old man rose out of his seat and stood, wobbling, ever so slightly.

The attention once again shifted to him. He stood and had a wonderfully goofy grin on his tired old face. His glasses sparkled with the bright colors from the fire and the glowing decorations.

He froze for just an instant, gathering his attention; he took a step with his bare right foot, and stopped again. I could see the gears churning in his bald little head, and then quickly he pulled the scrawny, white foot back. This time he tucked it in neatly with both of his heels touching. Slowly, Pa raised his arms like a child trying to fly or emulate an airplane. His arms rose and then "clicked" once they were level with his shoulders. He stood there with his arms stretched out and then he snapped his right fingers. We all laughed at the curious sight.

Then, once again, out came his right foot as if he were going to walk to the kitchen, then again he pulled it back and out shot his left foot. This time the toe was pointing and the heel was showing air. He snapped his fingers again.

"Pa," someone asked, "do you need something? Do you want me to get you something?" He just smiled and then reversed his footing in a quick shuffle and again he snapped his fingers.

"I think he's dancing," someone commented, and we laughed.

Pa pulled his arms in at that comment and then, like one of Gladys Knight's Pips, did a smooth, groovin' move to his left, leading with his hip. At the end of the step he flourished with a handclap. Then he did the same move to his right, stepping on crumpled paper as he went. One of my aunts became concerned for his safety and made her way closer to her elderly father.

"Pa, that was very good," she told him, "but you need to sit down for a few minutes." She reached out her hand to take his elbow. My grandfather snatched her hand with the speed of light, took it and then pulled, knocking my poor aunt completely off balance and falling towards the frail, senile, old man. Just as we winced and were about to cover our eyes, he caught her in his right arm and leaned her back, face to face.

Then he said, "Thank you, my dear. That was enchanting." And then he kissed her! My aunt gasped and my grandfather smiled and we all stood and sat in silence.

As I recall, the radio was playing "Jiggle Bell Rock" and my grandfather sang to my aunt, ". . . That's the jiggle bell, that's the jiggle bell, that's the jiggle bell rock . . ." and then he pulled her up and twirled her away.

At the time, my mother had a large wooden and metal coffee table in the center of this room and it was positioned just in front of the chair my grandpa had previously occupied. With my aunt spinning off into the arms of family members and recovering her composure, my grandfather leapt like Errol Flynn onto the big low table. That was enough! I put my kids on the floor and sat up. My uncles all rushed to the middle of the room encircling the coffee table. Each, in turn, reached for the old man who would laugh and dance and spin to keep out of their clutches.

"Santa Baby" came on the speakers and the old man began a wonderful Marilyn Monroe and the men lowered their guard and their arms, as they watched the old blacksmith dip his shoulders, turn his head, and sing sultrily towards his back. He winked at the men and pranced about acting as if he caressed a mink stole. He tossed his invisible, curly forelocks back out of his line of sight, "poo-poo, pee-do."

"Grab him, Jimmy," my mother shouted.

"Get him down before he gets hurt!" my Aunt Pat yelled to the men.

So, my father reached up slowly towards my grandpa. "Come on down, Pa, you're scaring the girls," he said warmly. The other men closed ranks around my grandfather's impromptu stage, and he realized he was trapped.

But capture, confinement, and caged subservience was not on the old man's list of things to do. It was an extremely fast movement, but for some reason I always recall the details in slow motion, for at this "moment of truth" my grandfather reached up and took the blades of the spinning ceiling fan in his grip. He bent his knees and lifted his feet and spun around the room laughing like a kid on a swing. Around and around he went, and I could see his flashing smile as he revolved.

I want you to know that I am not the kind of man prone to exaggeration for the sake of cheap entertainment, so you must believe me when I tell you that my grandfather released his hold on the churning blades, and like the world's greatest gymnast flew over the heads, arms, and open mouths of my shocked uncles and brothers. The women all screamed and the children were frightened as he flew, feet first, across the room.

My grandfather landed in a crouched kneeling position near the piano with his arms outstretched and his palms displayed. "Mammy!" he cried.

My grandfather rose and looked at us, smiled, tipped his hat, and then dashed in an instant out the front door. We stared at one another in utter disbelief and watched my grandfather through the window as he ran across fresh snow in the front yard, tearing off his good green Christmas sweater as he fled. Into the street he went, where he stopped briefly and turned to face us.

"Pa! Pa!" someone yelled.

"Oh my God, he's in the street barefoot!" one of my aunts cried.

We all moved to the front entrance and crowded on the porch. My father walked to the edge of the walkway in an attempt to catch him, but my grandfather clearly had an early lead. "Pa, come on back in and let's have some pie," my mom called out almost in tears. My grandfather smiled warmly, bowed to us, turned slowly and ran into the alley where he disappeared from our view.

The local police were called and the search continued for three days. Tracking dogs were called in and helicopters scoured the frozen streets, but they found nothing. News stations flashed his picture and we offered a reward for his return, but it was no good, he was gone. There was no trace of him (other than his good pocket watch that was found in the snow in the alley across from my parents' house). That was the last time I saw my grandfather.

In the late summer of the next year, just as my family slowly accepted the fate of our beloved patriarch and the cruelty and uncertainty of this mortal world, a friend of mine called late one Sunday night.

"Hey, I took the kids to the circus today," my friend Gary said.

"Cool. I heard it was in town," I answered.

"Listen man, this might sound kinda weird, but I think I saw your grandfather there." There was a long silence.

"Whadda you mean?" I followed.

Gary cleared his throat and laughed nervously. "Man,

this guy — your grandpa, was in the show!"

"Very funny," I said.

"No, I mean it man. He was doing a trapeze act!" Gary exclaimed.

I hung up the phone and haven't bothered to call Gary since.

I didn't want to say anything to Gary, but I had heard such rumors before. Grandpa in the Denton Community Theater's presentation of *The Fantastiks*, my grandfather doing a stint with the Blue Man Group in Laughlin, Nevada, and my sad personal favorite: the first Anglo ever invited to join the prestigious dance ensemble, the Harlem Ballet.

I don't understand the flaw in human nature that would make a person want to make up such a vicious and torturous lie. If I live to be a hundred, I'll never know what could possibly be their motivation in such a verbally abusive act? In a morbid way though, I do find some of the sightings somewhat amusing: co-starring in the remake of *Saturday Night Fever* with John Travolta. Give me a break.

I don't know, it's a little crazy, I guess. In the big picture, I guess maybe my grandfather's disappearance wasn't all that bad in some strange, hopeful way.

Maybe you shouldn't let people tell you that a certain thing can't be done. Maybe my grandfather is living proof.

Now, like anyone, I can certainly appreciate a good pair of cooperative socks. Good socks, socks that remain straight in their seams and nice and even at the top — as they should be. But if your socks are unruly and occupying too much of your time, maybe you should consider taking them off.

WHEN THE BIG ONES FALL

1

Life is funny sometimes. It's always weird and occasionally interesting. Life can be sad, but it always has the lingering aftertaste of sweetness.

Life *and* death fascinate me. It's one of my favorite flavors. I find the patterns of reality and sometimes lack thereof to be an unending source of awe and entertainment. I wait anxiously "wondering what strange side alley of human experience" my pursuits will lead. Some things come and some things go, and some things remain the same. The second law of thermodynamics basically states that if you leave stuff alone, it'll screw up. Another way of stating it: if there's *any* chance that something can go wrong, it will. My friend Murphy knew this well. Sometimes I like to sit and watch it go wrong, but usually I'm just sitting.

At Thanksgiving last year, Patti (my wife at the time) got this bright idea that we should go to Northern California and visit my brother and his wife who live there in the woods somewhere. Don't get me wrong, yeah, I love my brother and all that gooey stuff, but we don't feel the need to call each other and slobber all over the phone every decade like a bunch of girls or something. Actually in the last twenty-five years, I can't recall *either one of us* ever calling the other to say "Howdy." Okay, so maybe four phone calls a century wouldn't be asking too much, but it seems to work just fine for us. 'Cause, like dude, what is it they say? "Absence makes the heart grow Honda," ya know?

So now she wanted to go to California.

I just smiled and said, "Great!" knowing the day would never really roll around, or maybe I'd luck out and die before it occurred (Have you ever met anybody from California? They smell kind of funny, don't you think?). Have you ever known anybody that says they're going to do something, AND THEN they actually do it? Don't you just hate those kinds of people?

I couldn't believe it but Patti started making plans to go to California, non-refundable tickets and everything. As the months went by, I became slightly concerned as to exactly *how* I was going to get out of this. The death card had some real advantages, but I had too much work to do to die right then. It was just not an option at the time. Maybe God would intervene. Maybe I could buy the state and just have it shipped here, but that proved unrealistic. Maybe some terrorist would come through for me. For a while it looked like the airline was going to go under and I did the moonwalk whenever the news looked promising, but then those damn scab flight attendants screwed that one up. Thanks guys, I hope you're happy with your "security," and your "insurance," and making your "mortgage payments" at my expense. I guess some people can't seem to think about anybody but themselves.

You know, it's not just the plane-thing, it's the logistics of the whole mess also. As I'm sure you are aware, I have a special handicap that makes getting around a bit more difficult for me than for most people. You've probably already seen me on Oprah or Larry King, but in case you haven't, I'll take just a second to explain for the benefit of my readers that are unaware. I was born with a conjoined twin that was meant to be an identical twin, but something went wrong in the last few months of my mother's pregnancy. The doctors think it had something to do with a Super Glue commercial she had worked on as a young girl. And thus, we (my twin and I) have been joined since birth at the shoulder (my left, his right). We had learned to adjust our lives around our disability pretty well until about two years ago when Elbert, my twin, drowned during a water-skiing accident (I remember the phone call from the sheriff's office as if it were yesterday). So as you can imagine, it's a pretty big pain in the ass to do almost anything with a one hundred eighty pound corpse hangin' off your shoulder. But try as I may, it was beginning to look bad. I didn't want to get on an airplane. I hate to fly. I didn't want to leave my home. I didn't want to sit at a table and try to think of things to say to my brother and his wife of twenty-five years. I mean after all, really, we barely knew one another.

2

Isn't it funny? One fine day everything seems just great. It's April, the sun is shining, and the flowers are in bloom. Everything is perfect. You cruise down the alley in your wheelchair picking up aluminum cans. "Could it get any better than this?" you ask yourself. You eye your neighbor's piles of garbage, noting the good stuff for retrieval later, and then POW! The show's over, your mom flicks the porch light and you have to go home. It happens to everyone at some point.

When the ambulance arrived, my younger brother Kelley told us our father was still conscious and capable of speech. My dad was in a full-blown argument with the paramedics. Everything was okay, my father insisted, and they should butt out and let him get on with his can collecting.[1] After all, this was Sunday morning, and a big day was expected at the car wash near his home. All those beautiful cans would go to waste or worse yet, some

---

[1]Statisticians have estimated that over the course of his lifetime, my father had reclaimed over $28 in aluminum cans alone.

homeless person (or similar thief) might beat him to the spoils.

They rushed Daddy to Parkland Hospital anyway. Parkland is the serious Dallas County facility that has a world-class trauma unit, so it's not a good omen if you're the freight they're haulin' in the back of an ambulance.

Kelley called me and left a garbled message on my voicemail. When I got the message I called our older sister Susie. We all met at Parkland within the hour and the prognosis was not encouraging. My mother was calm, but I think she was wearing her filters that only heard things the physicians had to offer that were optimistic.

A CAT scan revealed my father had a broken blood vessel in his brain. It was on the right side of his brain, so the left side of his body was inversely affected from the fluid build-up. The bleed was so massive and the pressure was so great that it was pushing over the corpus callosum and distorting the left hemisphere as well, so the right side of his body was out of action also. It was deep in the brain tissue, so drainage wasn't a good option. The bottom line was, short of a miracle, things appeared grave. It was a tough day for us. I don't really know if it was a tough day for my dad.

On Tuesday we were told to come to the hospital as fast as we could. He went quickly and quietly and painlessly. He never regained consciousness. I asked the doctors if I could be in the room with him when they did the test to determine brain death. The nurse looked at me as if she *knew* that I was crazy, but I think the doctor could tell I would be okay. I stood quietly by the door and watched. I just wanted to be near him. I didn't find it ugly or upsetting or anything like that. On the contrary, I found it quite settling. The part of the human brain that makes us human is found in the cerebral cortex. That's where speech and memory and motor skills and things like that are housed. That was the area of my father's brain that was initially affected. As the pressure increased, it spread disruption to other portions of the brain and the system began to close up shop.

Now, the brainstem is one of the oldest organs in our cognitive evolution. A lot of our animal brethren share this feature with us. It's the primal brain in us, it doesn't think, it *does*. Its actions are so basic that these reactions are called "involuntary functions." It controls the mechanisms that make our bowels "milk" (or push) matter in the correct direction. It makes our hands pull away from fire. It controls the rhythm of our heartbeats and our breathing. It's out of our control.

The test is very simple. First, the hospital obtains a signed release order not to resuscitate. The medical staff then removes all forced life support and all respirators. Then they just watch you. They stand there for six minutes and just watch you. If you don't take a last dying gasp for air in those six minutes, then you're dead.

My father did not gasp.

3

I would like, if I could, to borrow a small piece of *your* life that I know I can never return, to selfishly tell you a little about this man who was such an influence on my life.

His name was James, but everyone called him Jimmy. He loved to fish. He was funny and sweet and always there when you needed him. He was a Marine in World War II and although he was at Iwo Jima, I don't think he ever *really* hated the Japanese. He was a welder and a cripple. He was a momma's boy, and he never once touched a cigarette or took a drink of alcohol. He was a big man. He was a pool hustler. He was an amazing athlete when we were both younger, and he loved any kind of sport. He was handsome. He was modest. I never saw him read a book or a magazine, but don't think for a moment that he wasn't smart, because he NEVER argued with my mother.[2] I don't think he ever went to a movie in my lifetime. The only plays I think he ever saw were the ones that myself or other family members were in. And of course, he was a world-class recycler.

When he was a young boy, he glued a bunch of marbles he had won to a piece of wood in the shape of a star, he then donated it to the kids at Buckner Orphans Home at Christmastime. As an adult, it broke my heart when I learned that my father had had to spend some time there himself as an orphan.

Also, he built me a wooden fort for my cowboys and Indians out of apple crates he had gathered from behind the grocery store. He used beads to make the doorknobs for the little doors. Other parents saw it and hired him to build copies for their children, but mine was the best.

In the mid 60's, "Stingray" style bicycles were too cool. They had tall handlebars and banana seats, but they were very expensive. So my dad made me one. It was the best bike I ever owned.

He stood up for me to my mom and explained how beneficial he thought violin lessons would be for me in the fifth grade. Later, he stood up for me to my mom and explained how beneficial he thought it would be for me to drop out of violin lessons in the fifth grade.

He understood that I was puny and not interested in sports. That was just fine with him. He never pushed. Instead he sang old Mills Brothers' songs with me in the car when we were alone.

He talked my mom into getting me the best guitar in the window. He talked my mom into getting me the best piano on the showroom floor. There were no lectures and

---

[2]Well once, circa 1964, he and my mother argued one evening and it scared me so bad that I called the police. The two cops got a look at my father and decided they didn't want any part of my parent's disagreement.

no questions. He always just seemed to want what I wanted. Isn't that unusual?

The batteries that ran the universe went dead one Sunday, and by the time they were changed, my father was gone.

4

Later in the spring, we sent my dumb-ass, alcoholic neighbor Karl off to Minnesota to dry out. I had to take him to the airport. I didn't want to forget this appointment so I wrote in large, red, block letters on the calendar in my office:

5/13/02, TAKE KARL TO RE-HAB

Karl's time had finally come, and *my* day finally came too. I woke up early on May 23, smoked eight cigarettes, took a handful of sedatives and flew to Sacramento. The flight took three hours, then I set my watch back two hours, so I almost got there before I left, but it sure felt like I was in the plane for three hours, weird huh?

We drove up to a little town north of Redding called Dunsmuir. Dunsmuir was originally called Pusher.[3] Then one day about a hundred years ago, a guy got off the train there and said, "This is a pretty little town. Why don't you name it after me?" And the people in the town did. The guy got back on the train and never came back.

Dunsmuir was okay, if you like laid-back. They have a cool, old movie theater there, but it was closed. They had a pretty neat-looking little bar on Main Street, but we were warned, "I wouldn't go in there." Everybody there seemed to either work for the railroad or grow pot for the guys that worked for the railroad. All in all, very uneventful.

We met my brother and his wife Diane at one of the

---

[3]Oh, by the way, the next town up from Pusher is Weed. And I can't really remember, but I think the next town after that is called Crack Pipe.

local restaurants for dinner. It was great food and I enjoyed watching the locals. It's strange, but they even have fat hillbillies in California. I saw American flags there, too! Some people smoked cigarettes and drove forbidden automobiles. And listen, when no one's looking, these guys in California eat at McDonald's just like the rest of us. Where were those California babes? Where was O.J.? I demanded to see Jack Nicholson immediately. This was bullshit, man!

The next day we went up into the mountains and Patti photographed a frozen lake that had been formed by a glacier carving a large indention in solid granite. Because there was so little soil there was an absence of plant life, and in turn no aquatic life. It was kind of sterile, I guess. Patti liked it though, so I guess everything in the world is just fine.

All the rest of the "family-pack" had done this lake thing (called Castle Crag) at dawn, but I don't do sunrises anymore. Besides, I saw one just a few years back on my way home one morning. Ooh, sunrise, big deal.

Mount Shasta was kind of interesting. I mean, here we were cruising around in shorts with the windows down, and the next thing that we know we were talking to some guy on the top of a mountain in a six-foot snowdrift.

My older brother and his wife invited us to their home one night for dinner. They live right on the Sacramento River, way up there in the mountains. He could draw you a map but you still couldn't find it. See, you cross the river, then you turn right and when the road ends, THEN you just keep going. You'll see a sign that says, "Caution! Turn back, don't try to be a hero," but just keep going. Within just a few miles, if you're persistent, you'll see a pack of wild dogs chasing you. Now here, you just have to keep going, because there's no room to turn around. My older brother and his wife are right there to your right. They're right *there,* to your right, up on the hill, in the trees, waving, holding a cup of freshly brewed coffee, twenty-four hours a day (Open Memorial Day).

We got there about eight or nine o'clock and looked the place over. It was all decked out with little colored lights hanging from the trees. They easily had an acre of front yard and it was full of blooming flowers, shrubs, and clinging vines.

My favorite part was the trees. They had Douglas fir, cedar, redwood, and an array of other less noble specimens on their property. Some of these things were at least four-foot in diameter. They were massive, spellbinding things. I figured they were probably about thirteen feet around. I'd never seen a tree that large before. My brother said the average age of his larger trees was between three hundred and four hundred years old.

It seemed to me that people in Northern California didn't take things all that seriously. Have I mentioned that they're laid-back? Well anyway, they're pretty laid-back, or either they're just too stoned to sit up and look around occasionally. They seem to enjoy sitting and watching the river go by for days. And sometimes they get to see stuff float by. I guess it's one way to pass a lifetime, but it's not for everybody.

With this depreciation and devaluation of time eating at our thoughts, Patti and I stole glances between us, as we became more and more aware of the fact that our evening meal was not going to make it *this* particular evening. We talked and looked around, and talked a little more. We tried to "lay-back," but we couldn't quite get it right. First ten o'clock then eleven o'clock passed uneventfully, with only the rumblings of Patti's stomach to break the silence of the sleeping forest.

I really thought for a moment that it was Bigfoot crashing down the hill through the trees to kill us all; except maybe, he might have possibly spared me. With my dashing good looks and the refinement of a classic "Renaissance Man," I'd hoped he might have chosen to keep me alive to serve as his mentor and mate.

"Do you need some help getting the grill going?" I asked my brother, hoping to see my watch in the dim light.

"No, it's cool. I got it," he answered, looking up at the blackness of the sky.

We finally ate and made it back to town. We hit the road the next day, where I could once again rely on the comforts of *real* strangers.

We drove south past Lake Shasta (Canadian for *feminine* or *French-like*) to Redding, then turned west towards the coast. They got *some* stuff in California I guess, you know, oceans and mountains and vineyards and stuff like that, so it wasn't all *that* bad.

In the tiny town of Redcrest, tucked somewhere up in the woods of Northern California, I ate breakfast one morning and left the diner to go for a short stroll and see the town. There wasn't much to see, so I just nodded at the locals and smiled like I was having a good time. Under an old modular carport I read the words "First Response Unit." It was a piece-o-crap station wagon with years of dust atop it. They had even BACKED IT IN like it was a rocket, set to blast off at the first hint of smoke. Someone had thought at one time that this tired old Pontiac was going to make a difference: ". . . A new weapon in the battle of the elements. You folks back there should stand clear. She's spring-loaded and ready for action . . ."

I walked over to the poor thing with a grin on my face, and peered inside to check out all their specialized gear and hi-tech gizmos. It was full of boxes stuffed with duct tape. I could hear the survivors' voices in my mind: "Supercar, you made it!"

I guess I met some nice people there also, and I got to see some of their underwear in the hotel laundry facilities. I stumbled into a bar in Eureka (Italian for "I found a good bar") and found it to be nice and seedy. Patti and I sat and spoke with the natives and exchanged phone numbers and email addresses when we parted. One young woman I was talking to earlier in the evening politely insinuated that I might be a bit "shallow and superficial," but she was overweight, so what she thought didn't count.

Oh yeah, if you're heading down towards Fort Bragg or Mendocino and you're wondering where to stay, don't let the name Fort Bragg fool you, it's not just for breakfast anymore. It's a great little town with an interesting downtown, and an actual working wharf district that's full of local color and best of all — sea lions. They are cute and they interact with humans in a curious way. I didn't even want to kill them.

I saw an old pickup truck there with a bumper sticker that read "Recall Gray Davis." I roared. Oh yeah, like *that* was ever going to happen. Who would they elect in his place, Sylvester Stallone? Those wacky, dumb-ass Californians, you just gotta love 'em, don't ya? And what about Mendocino, you may ask? Well, the nicest thing I can say about *it* is that it sucks, and I don't mean that in a good way either. I'd be willing to bet that anyone that says otherwise has a bow in her (or his) blonde hair. It's a Gucci of former L.A., whores and their recent captives gone dull. We decided to split after lunch. I had the lead-fish with a very heavy mercury sauce. Patti ordered a bowl of — I think the waitress called it "toad food."

The next day we headed up to the Redwood National Forest to see, guess what — more trees! I was so excited. Did you know the ranger station is on the coast? It sits out in a bunch of boring sand dunes with the stupid, flat, gray ocean taking up half the view. I thought, "Oh great. I'm sure *this* is going to be real entertaining."

"Is this forest underwater?" I asked Patti. "You know I don't like underwater forests." But she just left me sitting there as she walked into the information center.

5

The very *second* we pulled into the park I saw a thirty-story building disguised as a piece of wood. I saw through its masquerade instantly, as I knew there was no such thing.

I don't know if there is any way in my limited vocabulary that I can express the awe and wonderment I felt when I first saw a "big one." "Holy shit!" was all that could emerge from my throat and I stopped the car in the middle of the blacktop.

"Holy shit," I repeated, "Is that thing real?"

I got out of the car and walked towards the monster. Friend, there were boats in there — great big boats. There were a thousand pianos hiding beneath the bark. There were ski lodges and eight million cuckoo clocks. Here was a living quarter-mile train trestle.

It was just standing there, half-sleeping, half-posing, and the other half couldn't give a rat's ass about its insignificant rodent-cousin at its base that was your humble narrator.

"You wanna piece of me, punk?" it asked. I just shook my head slowly from left to right.

"Get out of the road!" Patti yelled from the car.

But I just stood in the roadway with my mouth wide open and stared. It was like seeing *Fiddler on the Roof* on Broadway with Zero Mostel, the first time I saw Mesa Verde, or the Brooklyn Bridge. It was like meeting Einstein. It was watching Hendrix live. It was Bourbon Street. It was seeing what's-his-name's painting of George Washington crossing the Delaware, while Leo Kottke plays in the background. It was as strong as the Honor Guard that marches in rigid solitude at Arlington National Cemetery. It was better planned than the Great Pyramid of Giza. It was Cirque du Soleil, Emlyn Williams, Bob Dylan, Leslie West, and all the pleasures of the senses rolled into one gigantic log.

I couldn't have spoken coherently if I had tried. So I fell back to muttering my newly found mantra: "Holy shit."

It was the single most inspiring thing that I have ever seen.

Finally, the shock faded and dissipated. I began to look about. There were wooden skyscrapers *everywhere*: Titans' brooms, dusting away the clouds! To my left, I think they were even larger. To my right were legions. I was drawn to them, not believing my eyes. I walked down the lane looking first up and then around. Patti got in the driver's side and followed me slowly in the car. I must have walked four hundred yards. I also noticed that every single square inch of unoccupied space beneath these monoliths was densely carpeted with beautiful ferns. It was breathtaking to behold. It was the best movie set I had ever seen. "Who does work like this?" I asked myself.

"I want a picture of this!" I cried, pointing to an enormous specimen. Then a moment later, "No this one, this one right here. This one is my favorite tree in the whole world. I want to marry this tree!"

When you stand there hypnotized you can't help but be conscious of the fact that this brother of yours is the tallest living thing on earth, that you are so minute, uninteresting, and bland. This tree before me contained more mass per square foot of ground space than anything that has ever lived.

This was *Maximus treemoneous biggus* heaven.

The way I figure it, on about the third or fourth night, God must have had a few drinks and was just sittin' there flippin' the channels around. I bet He glanced over His shoulder to make sure no one was watching and decided to make a few of these wonderful things just for the heck of it. He really did it for Himself, I think. He didn't figure we'd ever have the depth to get it. Thanks, Dude.

The *real* title for this species of coastal redwood is *Sequoia sempervirens.*[4] They say its literal translation comes out "always green," but to me it would have been *more* accurate to say "forever living." It might even be the same thing. I think I would have named it this because — well they just

---

[4]Just a side note here that I find — coincidental? To me, the Latin name of the tree is similar to *Semper Fidelis* which means "always faithful." This of course, is the motto of the United States Marine Corps.

don't want to die, and they can prove it too. It is *hard* to kill these towering columns. They're rugged and damn near almost indestructible. They are not afraid and they won't back down. You know, you don't live 2500 years in a forest and not go through a myriad of forest fires and bar fights. Bugs can't eat them and you can't drown them. You can't even hurt their feelings.

I've seen redwoods with large rooms hollowed out in their trunks and green vibrant leaves above. There's a *living* tree that you could drive a limousine through. I walked into this particular tree to inspect the tunnel, but I was *blown away* when I looked up and found it was completely hollow! The bark alone must have transferred the necessary nutrients up and down the stalk to keep the canopy growing.[5]

There are a few other species of trees around the world that have similar DNA, but they just don't have the same stature or way with the ladies. They're really just a bunch of wanna-be punks if you ask me, and they need their asses kicked (and I'm just the guy to do it).

But to me, the most fascinating thing about these trees is when and how they fall. It was a mystery how something so grounded to the planet could just decide one day to go for it. More than half of the downed trees I examined showed no signs that their demise was caused by man. Why the ones felled by humans were still there, I knew not. It seemed such a waste.

One of these behemoths lying on the ground can stretch three hundred to four hundred feet in length. That's longer than a football field! They build roads and lanes *around* them. I've heard rumors that when a giant redwood falls, it can be read on the Richter scale. Curiously, when they do fall, they almost always break in sections that are thirty to

---

[5]Note to Editor: A tree's bark may not be what supplies the nutrient to the upper portions. I may be confusing trees with canines again. What kind of bark does a dogwood have? Let's find out please and correct this before publication, so I don't look like an idiot.

forty feet long. On their sides these sections have the same girth, height, and length as a single tanker car, so the overall appearance is not unlike that of a brown and green train of cylindrical cars, all lined up in the forest.

When they fall, the thick vegetation quickly climbs up from the forest floor and attaches itself to the tops and sides as they begin raising the next generation. Some of these decaying trees take thousands of years to return back to the earth. Occasionally, they are so overgrown that it's difficult at a glance to recognize them. Some people might not see them for what they really are. Though they rise too abruptly to be natural mounds or hills, one could overlook their presence and importance. I'm sure they fool some people. Dirt fills in the deep crevasses in the bark that faces towards the sky. It is not uncommon for these rough troughs to be ten inches deep or more, and when filled with wind-blown soil and other natural debris, they make perfect planting pots. The ferns and ivy flourish, and just as often, seedlings from the parent plant take root as well.

Coastal redwoods, unlike many varieties of trees, can propagate from *two* possible natural scenarios. This is but one more example of its tenacious desire to keep going. This may be its single greatest long-term survival asset.

One method of reproduction is of course the seed, which basically falls sooner or later from the parent. Some are eaten or fall prey to fungus or other parasites. Some seeds are blown in the wind or carried by other means to climates unsuitable for their growth. Some fall in the crack of a rock or in the road or river. Some are dormant and some, I guess, are just stupid. A few get into the earth and get all moved in and buy a new set of TV trays just to break through the ground and find they've landed in the dry sun, or under a fallen tree, or just become a tasty snack for some animal.

Fortunately, coastal redwoods can also regenerate by sprout. A sprout can pop up damn near anywhere on a redwood tree: the base, the trunk, or the limbs. A new tree can just grow right out of an old one. Even one that is almost dead. The parent tree supplies all the essential minerals and nutrients required for a reasonable chance at life for the sprout. Once the sprout is plugged into the host it can have the use of thousands of years of an established root system. It also gains the inherent immunities of the family. It is the heir to a family domain, kind of like you and me. They reminded me of my father.

These guys, these lovers of life, they feed and protect their young. The parent nurtures them until their roots are planted firmly and then they let them grow. Sometimes the young don't just grow near or next to the parent, but within it and stands proudly upon it. Looking at a young tree deep in the moist shade of the forest, Patti said, "I think it's so wonderful how a new tree just grows out of the dead ones."

"Yeah, me too," I thought to myself, "Thanks for everything, Daddy. I'll always love you."

I Think This Is When It All Ended

Well, I'm back in Dallas and I've picked up a cold somewhere in the last few days. My throat hurts and my ears are stopped up, so I think I'll go and lie down for a while. Maybe when I get up we can make some strawberry cupcakes with cream cheese icing. Doesn't that sound good? But I think right now is about the hour "when a man gives his first yawn and glances at the clock" for me.

I regret not being able to find an appropriate place to add the line, "The road to Heaven surely passes through Mexico (sometimes I stop there to get gas)."

I guess you've probably already figured out that some of this stuff was written while I was under the influence of alcohol. Most of it was written under the guidance of mood altering drugs; even worse, some of it was conceived and undertaken while I was just sitting here being just the way I was built.

You're welcome and goodnight.

Fishing with God

Coda
⊕

One day my father and God were fishing. They had found a great spot alongside a softly moving stream. The sun was warm and there were a few nice, cool willow trees to stand under whenever they wanted a little shade.

Suddenly God's cork bobbed and then went under the surface. The Lord made a quick snap upwards with His pole and snagged the fish. My father (being the better fisherman) offered his advice on the best way to land the catch. God reeled in the fish, reached out, grabbed the taut line, and pulled the fish out of the brook. My father and God were both pleased and the Lord held the little guy up to His eye-level.

"Nice," my father said. God grinned and nodded.

Then God brought the fish closer to His face. "Curtis?"

"Arg," answered the fish, displaying much difficulty in his articulation with the hook still protruding from his mouth.

"Oh, sorry," God said and removed the hook from the fish's mouth. "Curtis, man, how you been?"

"Cool. Everything's been great," the fish answered.

"I almost didn't recognize you, you've grown so much," the Lord stated, beaming with pleasure.

"Yeah, it's been a while."

God held the fish up towards my dad. "Jimmy, I want you to meet an old friend of mine. This is Curtis."

My father nodded. "Hello."

God then turned his attention back to Curtis. "How's Carol?"

"Oh, she's just great."

"And the kids?"

The fish smiled. "Man, you know, just getting bigger every day."

God grew solemn and He quietly inquired, "And little Bob? How's he, is he doing better?"

Curtis brightened up with obvious pride. "He's really doin' good these days. I think the worst is behind him, thanks for askin'."

"Good, good," God nodded.

"Hey," Curtis asked politely, "is it cool if I split now? Carol's having friends over this afternoon."

A little embarrassed, God said, "Oh yeah, sorry. It's just been such a long time since we've had time to talk."

"So I'll check you later then, man," Curtis said.

"Yeah, be cool Curtis," God followed, and then tossed

the fish back into the peaceful water. God and my dad watched him swim away.

My father and God fished for a few minutes in silence. For some reason my father's thoughts turned to me and he became a little sad as he stood there gazing at the blue water. Something about the encounter between God and Curtis had sparked a sad memory. The Lord could tell something was upsetting my father, but He held His tongue.

Finally, my father turned towards God who was watching His cork floating along the smooth surface.

"Hey, God," my father began, "what about my son?"

"Hmm?"

"Do ya' ever hear anything about him?" my dad wondered aloud.

God just smiled and drew in His pole and leaned on it for a moment. "Yeah, he's fine, Jimmy." My father nodded his head.

"I've got a pretty good handle on things and I'm watching him for you," God concluded with subtle authority. My dad nodded his head again and tried to smile, but he was still concerned about my life on earth.

Finally God said with a grin, "Ya know, I've always liked that fish Curtis," God proclaimed pointing out at the water. "He's a good creature, and I love him. And I love his family too, but you know Jimmy — man, he's just a fish." That made both the Lord and my father smile. An hour later my father caught a six-pound bass named Raymond.

Delbert lives in a small town outside of Dallas, but usually spends most evenings in the bars where he enjoys sitting and listening to other people talk. He occasionally still trains Navy Seals when they really need it. He is real good-looking and is an excellent dancer (both modern (mostly hip-hop) and classic). He likes The Bee Gees (but not for their music) and his favorite food is chicken tenders. Stephen King has owed him $7.00 for a while now, so if you know Mr. King, you might want to let him know that "It's about to hit the fan" if this debt is not cleared up soon.

DIESELPUNK:
AN ANTHOLOGY

available now!

Available in both print and ebook format

Visit www.TwitPublishing.com for more details!

Praise for *The New Orleans Zombie Riot of 1866*

"Craig Gabrysch has created a fantastic Weird Western series . . . Keep an eye out for this book from Twit Publishing."
Westernpunk - The Weird, Wicked, and Wild West

"With one leg straddling the line of Old West adventure and the other deep in the kind of crawling horror you would find the Cthulhu Mythos, the stories are in turn thrilling, chilling, and with a fair bit of wicked humor thrown in to cut the tension."
David DeMar, Author of "Blowing off Some Steam"

Look for it in print and ebook on Amazon.com

Twit Publishing

Comic Books. Novels. Short Stories. Media.

Want to find out more about Twit Publishing?

Then go to www.TwitPublishing.com

Read about the company, hear about upcoming releases, and find links to our authors.

* * * * * * *

You can also find us at:

www.Facebook.com/TwitPublishing

www.TwitPublishing.WordPress.com

and

www.Twitter.com/TwitPublishing